SUTTON'S SINS

THE SINFUL SUTTONS BOOK 2

SCARLETT SCOTT

Sutton's Sins

The Sinful Suttons Book 2

For more information, contact author Scarlett Scott.

www.scarlettscottauthor.com

CHAPTER 1

LONDON, 1816

*R*afe woke, as he often did, with a woman in bed next to him. Nothing at all out of the ordinary in that regard.

No, indeed. It was not the bed that was the problem, though it was a mite small.

Nor was it the aching in his head, which was damned unpleasant, he would not lie.

Nor, even, was it the fact that he was naked without recalling a single moment of the glorious fucking he must have enjoyed the night before. Though, to be fair, that *was* a disappointment.

The true problem was that he did not know where the floating hell he was.

The room was unfamiliar. Small and spare. That in itself was hardly remarkable. But the carpet was fine. And the windows were large. The light coming in around the edges of the curtains landed in the hair of the slumbering female at his side. Blonde-red, that hair. A truly beautiful color, a combination of fire and gold, like a sunset.

A *sunset?*

What a sapskull. He hoped he was still cup-shot. 'Twould be the only excuse for thinking such tripe.

But the woman's hair was unique and lovely. He didn't think he had ever seen another shade quite like it, and Rafe had seen a great many ladies with their hair unbound.

He took up a long curl and twirled it around his finger, wondering who she was. Her back was to him, the bedclothes tucked neatly around her as if they were a protective shield. And for the first time, he took note of something else. She had her own counterpane separate from his. That was damned odd. She was swaddled like a babe, as far from him as possible. There was also a pillow separating them.

Hmm.

Rafe pulled back his portion of bedclothes to confirm he was as naked as he felt. Nary a stitch. Had his bedmate belatedly acquired modesty? Careful not to wake her, he gently hooked her counterpane with his forefinger and drew it back to reveal her shoulder.

She wore a crisp-white night rail trimmed with lace. When was the last time he had bedded a woman and she had donned a garment, rolled to the edge of the bed, and placed a pillow between them as if it were a defensive wall?

Grimacing, he tucked the coverlet back into place and then scrubbed a hand over his face. Had he been an arse? Displeased her in some way? Who was she, and where was he?

Suddenly, the haze leached from his mind. Memories tumbled over themselves. The day before had been steeped in madness, quite literally. His brother's wife, Lady Octavia, had nearly been killed. Together, Jasper and Rafe had rushed to Jasper's new town house, and they had found Octavia suffered from a slash to the throat. The surgeon had been called, the madwoman responsible for the heinous deed taken away by the charleys, and Rafe had been left watching over his twin nieces, Anne and Elizabeth, along with their new governess. He remembered finding the brandy after his sister-in-law had been patched up.

Surely he had not…

Nay, he would not have been so depraved, he was sure. And if the governess had possessed such unique hair, he would have taken note. But suddenly, he recalled that all her hair had been tucked away in a hideous cap.

Still, he would not have bedded his nieces' new governess, would he?

Rafe struggled to remember, but his mind was blank as a starless sky. There had been brandy with the governess—Miss Bird was her name, he thought—and then nothing after. The name did not seem right. Not Miss Bird. Something else. Miss Hen?

A scratching sounded at the door. "Miss Wren?"

Christ! The voice belonged to one of his nieces. He could not tell the twins apart, not by sight, and most certainly not by voice. Was it Elizabeth or was it Anne? He supposed it hardly mattered. He could not run the risk of them waking the woman whose bed he was currently occupying. It was imperative she remain asleep until he figured out just what the hell had happened.

Jasper was going to give him a sound drubbing if he had indeed tupped the governess.

Gathering the bedclothes around him like a shroud, Rafe rose from bed. He padded to the door in his bare feet and softly opened it. Two curious sets of hazel eyes looked up at him.

"Uncle Rafe?" they asked in unison.

"Where is Miss Wren?" one of the girls asked.

"Why are you wearing a counterpane?" the other queried.

He grimaced. "She is sleeping and I… I am cold."

Predictably, his nieces began chattering.

"Why are you in her chamber?"

"I'm hungry."

"Elizabeth pulled my hair."

"I told you I was sorry," said that twin to her sister.

And at last, Rafe could tell who was whom.

He blinked, his headache thumping harder.

"Do not tell your papa you saw me in Miss Wren's chamber," he said, though he knew it was wrong to encourage his nieces to lie.

As if it were not enough that Rafe was wearing nothing but a counterpane and conversing with his innocent nieces while their governess, whom he may or may not have bedded, slept on, another creature bounded down the hall. His brother's youngest pup, Motley, approached the girls with a playful bark.

Damn it, what a muddle.

"Take the bleeding hound to see your papa, girls," he told them as Motley sprang forward and caught the corner of his counterpane in his sharp teeth. "Blast it, arsehole, leave me be."

"Come, Arsehole," Elizabeth said cheerfully, using the decidedly improper name the pup had inherited thanks to his poor manners.

Rafe winced. Jasper's wife would box his ears if she learned he was cursing around the girls. She had already warned not only himself but the rest of his brothers and all the men at his family's gaming hell, The Sinner's Palace, as well.

"Perhaps you ought not to repeat everything Uncle Rafe says," he muttered.

Or perhaps it would be more apt to say the twins ought not to repeat *anything* Uncle Rafe said. Ever. Most especially not anything he *did*.

Bedding their governess—if he had—would not have

been one of his more exemplary moments. But then, did he truly possess exemplary moments? Likely not any suitable for the ears of his innocent young nieces.

"Why are you cold?" Anne asked.

Because I am bloody well bare-arsed underneath this cursed blanket.

"Perhaps I'm ill," he lied without compunction.

"You don't look it to me," Elizabeth pronounced.

"Mayhap he's cropsick," Anne suggested to her sister, before turning a considering look back at him.

Twin pairs of hazel Sutton eyes swept over him from head to toe.

"Cropsick," he repeated, wondering how she knew the word to describe the pronounced affliction affecting a man the day after he had been as drunk as David's sow. "And where did you hear of that?"

"Uncle Hart and Uncle Wolf," the girls said in unison, making him wonder what else his brothers had been teaching their nieces. Nothing beneficial, he was sure.

Damn it all, he needed to put an end to this interview.

Now.

He cupped a hand to his ear, pretending as if he had heard something down the hall. "I do believe your papa is calling for you."

Motley began tugging on the counterpane and growling. Cursed mongrel. To think Rafe had often shared his supper with the traitor.

The girls turned away as if about to skip off at last.

"Wait," he bit out, jerking his counterpane free of Motley's persistent jaws. "Don't forget the hound." He pointed a finger at Motley and summoned his most commanding tone. "Off you go, beast."

Motley tilted his head and offered another deep bark.

Did no one in this bloody household listen to him?

He gritted his teeth, about to issue another command, when Elizabeth snapped her fingers at the dog.

"Come along, Arsehole," she said sternly.

"I thought I told you not to repeat Uncle Rafe," he reminded weakly.

"You need to brush your hair, Uncle," Anne offered helpfully.

Now he was being insulted by a mere stripling of six years of age. And this after a hound had nearly stolen the sole textile keeping him from being naked as a babe. After he had arisen in the bed of a governess with absolutely no memory of what had happened the night before.

This was not going to be the best damned day of Rafe Sutton's life. That much was for bleeding certain.

"Run along, the lot of you," he growled at his nieces and the furred menace.

Giggling with delight, the twins obeyed at last, scampering away with Motley trotting obediently at their heels.

Now, he was left to face the ramifications of his actions. Grinding his molars, he closed the door and turned to face Miss Hen.

Er, Wren.

Feign slumber, Persephone. If he thinks you are asleep, he is likely to leave and spare you the embarrassment of an explanation.

Footsteps neared the bed as she kept her eyelids tightly closed against the light of late morning. The brightness of the sun suggested she had overslept. A strange development indeed when there had been an unwanted man on the other side of the pillow wall she had built to separate herself from his body. From his *naked* body.

Do not think of his body. Nay, you must not...

Too late.

She was recalling him as he had shucked his garments in an almost trance-like state, thanks to the laudanum she had given him in the hopes he would sleep. And he *had* slept. He was not formed like any other gentleman of her acquaintance, Mr. Rafe Sutton. Lean hips, broad shoulders, so much muscle, and good heavens, the forbidden place where her shocked gaze had lingered. The recollection of his long, thick hardness rising high was thoroughly unwanted, sending a flush from the soles of her feet to the roots of her hair.

Pray he does not notice, you hen wit. You have not ventured this far only to succumb to the whims of a charming scoundrel.

The steps drew closer. And with them came his presence. An awareness settled over her, one that was very much unwanted, along with a warmth she could not deny. Still, she took care to maintain deep, even breaths as if she were yet asleep.

Go away, she willed him. *Go far, far away. Take your charming grins and your handsome scoundrel's air and leave me.*

"Blast your top lights," he muttered.

Was he cursing her or was he cursing himself? She could not be sure. All Persephone could do was concentrate on her own slow, steady breaths. Eyes closed, nary a fidget. Remain still. Hope he would go away.

"The governess," he added. "You rutting bastard."

He was speaking to himself, then. Aloud. Strangely, she felt compelled to announce her lucidity. It was as if she were eavesdropping on a private conversation, which was wholly foolish in itself. There was no reason for her to hold Rafe Sutton's feelings in higher regard than her own. Nor was there a reason to admit she was awake, listening to all. She owed him nothing.

To be fair, perhaps she owed him a minor apology. After he had divested himself of his clothing, he had taken quite a spill, hitting his head on the narrow bedside table in the process. For a heart-shattering moment, she had feared him dead. But as she had rushed over his insensate form, he had emitted a long snore, chasing her frantic concern that she had unintentionally murdered the brother of her benevolent employer, Mr. Jasper Sutton. Wrestling him into the bed had been another matter, for he was a large man indeed.

"Miss Wren?"

The low, deep rumble of his voice sent a strange cacophony of sensation careening through her. Her wretched mind was busy dredging up thoughts of him from the previous evening when they had unexpectedly found themselves together, tending to his twin nieces. He had been...devastatingly charming. Too charming. He had disarmed her with that smile, those dimples and hazel eyes.

And he had been handsome, too, in a way she had never experienced before. He was not a dandy like Cousin Bartholomew, who was tall and elegant and prided himself on his elaborate cravats and the cut of his coats. Rafe Sutton was masculine and slightly disheveled and he wore sin as if it were a waistcoat. His blond hair was far longer than fashionable, with a curl that had made her long to run her fingers through it. The instinct had been both reckless and foolish, and she had promptly banished it.

"Miss Wren?"

This time, his query was accompanied by a gentle touch. Her shoulder, nothing more. Fortunately, she was tightly swaddled in her counterpane. She was also clad in a prim night rail which buttoned to her chin, but the extra layer of protection, keeping his skin from hers, was much appreciated even as his heat seemed to permeate the barriers, searing her.

"Curse it. You stupid, beetle-headed clod."

He was muttering to himself again now, and a foreign

bubble of laughter suddenly formed in her chest. There was something endearingly silly about this handsome rakehell—for if ever Persephone had seen a rogue, it was he—chastising himself aloud. *Beetle-headed.* She did not suppose she had ever heard the insult before. And now that she had begun to think about the phrase, the bubble grew larger, clawing its way up her throat before she could stifle it.

Her mirth fled her lips in a most distressing rushing of unladylike sound.

Giving her away.

Oh, Persephone.

"You're awake." His grim pronouncement meant she could no longer continue to lie still, ignoring his attempts at gently prodding her from sleep.

She opened her eyes to find Mr. Rafe Sutton hovering over her bedside, a coverlet wrapped around his shoulders in the fashion of a cape. Morning sunlight streamed around the edges of the curtains behind him, catching in his blond hair and giving the impression of a halo.

How foolish. There was nothing at all angelic about this man.

Or any man, for that matter.

She sat up, drawing the coverlet to her chin for modesty's sake. "You woke me."

That was a fib, of course. But better to prevaricate than explain she had been lying there, listening to his awkward discussion with the children. Listening to him call her name. Hoping he would simply give up and leave her alone. Or all the reasons why she had done so.

His gaze—an intriguing blend of gray, green, and brown—narrowed on her. "It's a bleeding miracle you were able to sleep through chattering twins and a barking beast."

Yes, it had been, but it was indecorous of him to point that out.

She frowned. "Nevertheless, I did."

He scowled. "Slumber like the dead, you do."

It was as if he did not believe her. And, well, he had every right to his suspicions. However, that did not mean it nettled any less. Particularly after the panic he had caused in her the night before. She knew she should not have slipped the laudanum into his drink. When he had begun staggering and slurring, she had seen the error in her rash decision. Her situation here in Mr. Sutton's household was yet new, and she did not doubt he would dismiss her in a trice if he suspected she had given his brother enough opium to lay a horse low.

She clutched the bedclothes tighter to her throat. "It is a fault of mine, sir. One of many."

Along with drugging him, but there was no need to make that admission aloud. She had felt guilty enough for her actions, and terrified she would lose her position, which she needed quite desperately.

"What 'appened?" he asked, the *h* notably missing from his speech, when he had previously spoken with an almost perfect, gentlemanly flair.

She supposed he was talking about the night before. Likely, his recollections would be rather...hazy. Best to feign ignorance.

"I have no notion of what you mean, Mr. Sutton."

His eyes narrowed even more. "I'm Abram. What do you think I'm speaking of, Miss Wren? The goddamn weather?"

Well, at last, she was witnessing a side of him that was not charming.

She blinked. "You are Abram? I must beg your pardon, Mr. Sutton. I thought your Christian name was Rafe."

He made a low sound in his throat, rather like a feral animal. "I'm not saying my name is Abram. It's flash for saying I'm naked. I was trying to keep your sensibilities in mind, you being a lady and such. *Are* you a lady?"

He did not mean *lady* in the sense she feared, she told herself, though her heart was hammering wildly and her mouth had gone dry.

"I am a respectable woman, Mr. Sutton," she said coolly. "If you are in *en dishabille*, the fault is yours. I was most distressed with your behavior last night."

He paled.

She knew the swift pinprick of guilt, then feverishly tamped it down.

"I didn't... *Hell*." He raked a hand through his tousled curls, the effect rendered somewhat comical by his attempt to hold the counterpane with one hand instead of two. He nearly dropped the right side, and the most shameless part of her would not have minded if he had one whit. "What happened between us, Miss Wren? Last night?"

Nothing was the proper answer.

Although, to be fair, that was rather concise. The truth was that he had been pleasant and charming, fretting over the welfare of his sister-in-law, Lady Octavia, who had been attacked by a madwoman and who had required stitching up by a surgeon. Thanks to the upended nature of the household, the two of them had been closeted away with Persephone's charges, attempting to distract them from the surrounding mayhem.

But after the girls had gone to sleep in the nursery for the evening, the attention he had paid her had triggered all the fears she had tried so hard to bury after what had happened at her last situation. She had panicked. Armed with the laudanum she had been carrying with her ever since that awful night, she had struck when Rafe Sutton had been distractedly pacing the salon. But she had given him far too much. Before her scattered wits had been able to comprehend what she should do to rectify her error, he swooped down upon her, taking up his glass. He had swallowed his brandy in a mad rush, the laudanum too.

But she could not tell him that. Because she needed this position. She needed to remain where she was.

Only without Rafe Sutton's interference and vexing presence.

"Miss Wren?" he prompted, waiting.

"You do not recall?" she returned, her mind whirling.

She needed to be certain he had no memory of the manner in which he had fallen so easily. If he were to go to his brother with concerns regarding her character...

She could not bear to think it.

"Of course I do not," he gritted. "If I did, I'd have no need to ask."

The sounds of other servants moving about could be heard in the hall, and her heart plummeted to her toes. It was one thing for the girls to have witnessed their uncle at her door—children could be easily bribed, she had discovered—but it was another for any of the domestics to find Mr. Rafe Sutton here in her room, alone and naked, with her.

"You must dress and go at once," she hissed, careful to keep her voice low lest any curious ears were listening near to the door. Her years of experience as a governess had taught her to expect anything.

He was frowning at her, his displeasure evident in the crinkle of his brow. "Miss Wren, I insist—"

"You have already done enough damage," she interrupted, fear making her throat go thick. "Dress and go before anyone else finds you here."

He regarded her, jaw clenched, stare impenetrable. And then, without a word, he turned away and set about hunting his discarded garments from the floor. On any other occasion, she would have laughed at the sight of this big, masculine man struggling to maintain his modesty in the counterpane whilst thrusting himself into yesterday's coat. But as the sun rose higher and the danger of discovery grew, all she could do was bite her lip and watch as he finished his hasty dressing and sent a glare over his shoulder in her direction, along with a warning.

"This is not the last you shall hear of this, Miss Wren."

He shrugged the counterpane to the floor. Where was his cravat? She could not say.

She told herself it was his warning that sent the shiver shuddering through her and not the sight of that strong, lean form, striding from her chamber.

But then, Persephone Wren was a dissembler, and she had been one for nearly the last seven years. That was hardly new. However, in the past, it had never been herself she had been deceiving.

CHAPTER 2

*H*aving been born to the rookery and lived all his life there, Rafe had never minded it. The stench was almost familiar. The danger, quite expected, if not appreciated. The desperation, an eternal reason to continue working one's fingers to the bleeding knuckles. And so it was, that as he returned to The Sinner's Palace after fleeing his brother's Mayfair town house with yesterday's togs—sans his damned cravat, which he had never found in his hasty search of Miss Wren's quarters—he inhaled deeply. A lungful of chamber pots, horse dung, and stale piss, as it happened.

With a slight tinge of sour wine and fish.

Of course, it was raining, which never helped matters much.

A flurry of movement at the edge of his vision caught his eye, and he turned, thinking he had spied the figure of a cove there. Hope rose that his brother Loge, who had gone missing, was still somewhere about. There had been the mysterious chap who had come to Lady Octavia's aid and then disappeared the night before to bolster this optimism, for he had resembled a Sutton. But the street was empty. Must have been his tired eyes playing tricks on him. With a sigh, Rafe trudged on.

When he reached the private entrance, he entered, passing by the guards and slipping into the hidden quarters of The Sinner's Palace. He and most, but not all, of his family —thanks to the marriages of his sister Caro and brother Jasper, their ranks had dwindled—dwelled within. Rafe removed his hat and coat, performing the same routine he had thousands of times before, wondering why today should feel differently.

It should not, he decided.

It *did* not.

He would forget all about Miss Wren and her sunset hair and warm brown eyes and that plump little mouth that begged to be kissed and the promise of lush breasts he had spied beneath her unappealing gown the evening before... Damn it, there he went again. Yes, the governess was undeniably what any man in the East End with a set of eyes would deem a *dimber mort*. In other words, a pretty wench. But he had seen—and tumbled—many pretty wenches. There was nothing different about this one. Well, nothing save the mystery of what had happened between them.

You have already done enough damage, she had said. Which rather begged the question. What damage? He knew he would never have forced a woman, regardless of how inebriated he was. But he had been naked. In her bed. Had he taken her virginity then? Was that the damage she spoke of?

Hell, he most certainly hoped not. Deflowering his brother's new governess was the work of a scoundrel.

On a sigh, he rounded a corner and collided with a chap wearing a hat pressed low over his brow. The unexpected jolt sent a spear of pain through his skull, reminding him that he had an aching garret. Curse it all, why did his head hurt so much? Rafe raked his fingers through his hair and discovered a knot on his scalp that was the source of the pain.

Surely Miss Wren had not bludgeoned him.

Had she?

"Oh dear," said the fellow into whom he had plowed, his voice familiar. "Forgive me."

Not just familiar, that voice, but feminine as well. Belatedly, it occurred to Rafe that the fellow was not a man at all. Rather, *he* was a *she*. And either he was well and truly addled in the upper story, or his sister Pen was wearing trousers and dressed as a cull.

"Pen?" he bit out.

"Damn," she muttered.

His younger sisters Pen and Lily had always been headstrong, but there was no denying that ever since Jasper had left the hell in favor of living in the West End like a bloody gentleman, they had been running even wilder. He supposed that in the absence of their family leader, he needed to step in. The realization was a novel one; he did best when he was free to be the ne'er-do-well of the family.

But since Jasper had started a family of his own, that left his siblings decidedly adrift. Which meant Rafe, the only brother currently standing in the hall, witnessing Pen's frolics, had to take action.

He pinned her with his most disapproving glare. "Penelope Sutton, what in the devil's arsehole are you doing running about the halls dressed as a cove?"

She blinked, then smiled with far more cheer than the situation merited. "I wasn't *running*, brother."

"Splitting hairs." He crossed his arms over his chest, trying not to allow the smile threatening to creep over his lips to do so. It wouldn't do for the minx to think he found her antics humorous. "You know damned well what I meant."

She sniffed. "If you must know, I was on my way to meet the gin merchant."

He raised a brow. "In such a fashion?"

"My gowns are in need of laundering."

He knew a lie when he heard one, damn it. "You've nary a single one that's clean?"

"Not one." She kept smiling, but she was shifting from foot to foot, as if she could scarcely wait to be free of his presence and questions.

Aye, he knew the signs. Hell, he was cut from the same cloth, and he had spent many a morning after a night of debauchery either avoiding or lying to Jasper about what he had done and where he had been. Which begged a question.

Why would she be dressed as a man at this hour of the morning?

"The gin merchant ain't coming today," he said, remembering that fact a bit belatedly, for their brother Hart often dealt with the merchants and their accounts. "Thursdays are the day when he shows his ugly face."

It was true—the gin merchant was an ugly, unscrupulous scoundrel. But by all that was holy and good, his jackey was fine.

"That is puzzling." Her smile slipped a bit. "Perhaps Hart had his days confused when he asked me to take his place."

Hart was sharper than a murderer's blade when it came to such matters.

"Or maybe you are lying," Rafe countered smoothly. "Where have you been, Pen? I don't want to tell Jasper about this adventure of yours, but I will if I 'ave to."

And hellfire, there he went again, losing his *h* like the lowborn rookery rat he was. As their circumstances had improved, Jasper had seen them all educated as best he could. To be sure, the Suttons were no lords and ladies. But they had done everything in their power to make The Sinner's

Palace one of the most well-known establishments in the East End. Along with the Winter family, they ruled supreme.

And what a rule it was.

"Rafe," Pen said, a plea in her voice and her eyes both. "There is no need to tell Jasper about seeing me dressed as I am. Please. You know how protective he is."

That nettled.

He raked his fingers through his hair and winced when he unintentionally connected with the sore lump once more. "And I ain't?"

What did you strike me with, Miss Wren?

It was clear he had some business yet to conclude with the fiery-haired woman.

"Of course you are protective." Pen patted his shoulder. "I hardly meant to say you aren't."

"I ain't one of Jasper's dogs. No need to pet me."

Or to attempt to distract him, which was what she was doing. He wasn't a green lad. He knew all the tricks, having employed them himself on innumerable occasions.

"I do miss Barnaby," his sister said with a sigh.

He missed Jasper's dogs as well, and he couldn't deny it. Well, mayhap not Arsehole. The scamp was always eating his boots, barking, or otherwise causing mischief.

"Get your own hound then," he suggested. "It ought to keep you busy enough that you aren't wandering about dressed like a lad and finding yourself in all manner of scrapes."

She tugged at the cravat she wore, pulling at the knot—a damned fine one, in his estimation. "Perhaps I will. But for now, I ought to at least make certain the gin merchant is not here."

"Scovey ain't here and you know it," Rafe countered. "Who taught you to tie such a fine knot?"

Doing so was an art. It had taken him years to perfect the

skill. A man had to at least play the part of a gentleman sometimes.

"I taught myself."

"Stop lying."

"I beg your pardon?"

"If you didn't 'ear me, maybe you should open your wattles," he suggested, perhaps unkindly.

Pen's shoulders went stiff beneath that ridiculous coat she was wearing. Christ, she had stuffed them with something to make herself seem larger than she was, and more masculine too. What the devil? Something suspicious was afoot.

"My ears *are* open," she snapped. "Why are you speaking flash?"

The answer was easy. "So you remember who and what you are. You're a Sutton, girl. As am I. You cannot fool me. Something is amiss here, and I won't stop until you admit it."

Someone had taught Pen to tie a proper cravat. *Someone* had been the reason she was sneaking about like a common thief, dressed as a cove and lying to her brother.

"And why should you think I'm trying to fool you, Rafe Sutton?" she demanded, planting her hands on her hips.

Now she was trying for outrage? Ha! He would not be distracted.

"Who?" he demanded curtly. "Give me a name. Tell me who the worthless fribble is. There has to be a gentleman involved. Am I wrong?"

She went pale. "Rafe, please."

"No secrets, Pen," he said, refusing to soften. "Suttons protect our own. Jasper ain't here, but I am. So you answer to me now."

And holy hell, but what a frightening realization *that* was. The responsibility of his siblings rested heavy as a boulder on his shoulders.

The breath escaped Pen in one big rush. She lowered her head, tucking her chin to her chest. "Luddaydenweer."

He blinked. "That makes no sense, sister. Speak slowly. *Concisely.*"

There was a fancy cull's word. One he had learned as a young man, when he had finally discovered how to read. Reading and tupping were his two favorite entertainments.

"Lord Aidan Weir," she repeated. "But you must not be angry with him, Rafe. Going to the matches has been my idea."

"Matches?" His scowl deepened. "You've been running about dressed as a cove with *Lord Aidan Weir*, attending boxing matches?"

He was more than familiar with Lord Aidan, who was the third son of a duke and an unrepentant rakehell. He had witnessed him at The Garden of Flora on more than one occasion, always with at least two of the ladies at that establishment hanging from his arms. Not the sort of chap a man wanted sniffing about his sister's skirts. By God, if the bastard had touched a hair on Pen's head, Rafe was going to punch him right in his lordly ivories. Hopefully, he'd knock out one or two...

Pen glanced up at him, wincing. "No need to yell, Rafe. It isn't as if we were going about picking pockets."

"Has he touched you?" he demanded, already plotting the drubbing he would deliver to Lord Aidan.

It hardly mattered that the man was a frequent and well-paying patron at The Sinner's Palace. Rafe would not stand idly by while some arrogant lordling defiled his sister.

"No, he has not," Pen said, shaking her head swiftly. "Why does no one believe me that we are friends?"

He narrowed his eyes, considering her. "Because lords like him aren't friends with a Sutton like you without him expecting something. You aren't to see any more of Lord

Aidan. The man is a lecherous scoundrel, and you'll not be tainted by 'im."

But Pen, being Pen, crossed her arms over her chest, taking on a mulish expression. "How would you know if he's lecherous? Lord Aidan has been a gentleman to me, quite unlike some lords I could name."

"No more dressing as a cove and no more sneaking about with that devil," Rafe told her flatly.

"You are judging him without knowing him," she countered, looking like one of Jasper's dogs when someone was trying to take his favorite bone. "If it were not for Lord Aidan, I would have been attending the matches on my own. Would you prefer that?"

Trouble. Sisters—and all females, really—were *trouble*.

This one especially.

"You aren't to go to the matches, Pen. It ain't a place for women. There's blood and violence and dangerous coves. You belong 'ere at The Sinner's Palace, tending to the ledgers and watching over Lily and the lads."

"Yes, of course I belong here, where it is convenient for you all to have me. I'll not hide away with the ledgers forever. I want freedom and adventure!"

Christ.

His head was throbbing now.

Curse you, Miss Wren.

"This freedom and adventure you speak of, Pen, it isn't what you think. Believe me. I know the sort of man Lord Aidan is. He's the sort who will bed you and forget you because you're a Sutton from the stews and he's the son of a duke. He'll leave you with a babe in your belly and not so much as a handful of notes and 'e won't look back."

"You're wrong about him," Pen defended.

Lord save him. He was going to have to talk to Jasper about this most unwanted development. And the rest of their brothers as well. Hart and Wolf would need to keep an eye on her and see that she wasn't free to roam about.

"I ain't wrong," he told his sister. "Trust me, Pen. I only want what's best for you. Now get to your rooms and change into one of your gowns before the men see you dressed this way."

"You're insufferable," she announced, and then she huffed past him like a storm blowing into the sea.

Well, perhaps she wasn't wrong about that bit. He couldn't deny it.

Rafe sighed and thought better of running his hand through his hair again, on account of that damned knot on his scalp. He would have to pay Jasper a call in Mayfair.

What a pity.

We shall meet again, Miss Wren.

CHAPTER 3

$\mathscr{P}$ersephone was in the small garden behind the town house, watching as her charges skipped happily about during this small break from their lessons. Their laughter bounced off the walls in a delightful echo that had her smiling. The unabashed joy Anne and Elizabeth radiated was catching.

Anne giggled and raced past Elizabeth.

Likely, Persephone ought to chastise them. To remind them they were ladies and they ought to move with grace and consideration instead of flitting like butterflies. However, her own experience with her governesses had left rather a sour taste in her mouth. The last, Wilkins, had been joyless and dour, and she had made every day a punishment rather than a gift. But then, so had Cousin Bartholomew.

Innocence was always spoiled.

Happiness was inevitably replaced with sadness.

It was her instinct to allow these sweet girls to bask in the elation of their youth and artlessness for as long as they could. She had not been so fortunate. Anne and Elizabeth were blessed with parents who loved and doted on them.

Persephone had been abandoned to the dubious care of others for as long as she could recall. But not even the isolated loneliness of her childhood could compare to what had come after.

"Where are my favorite twins?"

The masculine drawl at her back had Persephone jumping and pressing a hand to her madly thumping heart. When would she cease to think it was Cousin Bartholomew each time she was startled?

Not until she was truly free of him. That was the answer.

And anyway, this intruder was not her odious cousin. Rather, it was Rafe Sutton.

Again.

He prowled into the gardens like a dangerous beast. Handsome. Charming. Smiling his rogue's grin. *Sweet heavens above.* The gaze which was neither gray nor green nor brown flicked to meet hers and sent a jolt of awareness straight through her. Awareness she did not want, and which she was most certainly not meant to feel.

Her heart was skipping like Anne and Elizabeth, racing to meet their uncle.

"Miss Wren," he greeted with a courtly bow, which would have put any gentleman to shame.

She forced herself to dip into a curtsy in return, struggling to tamp down her body's foolish reaction to him. The reminder that he had spent an entire night in her bed, bereft of any garments, simmered beneath every passing second.

"Mr. Sutton," she offered, pleased with herself for keeping her voice so calm.

The girls threw themselves at him, each wrapping their arms around one of his legs. "Uncle Rafe!"

Their voices were in unison. As twins, their bond was strong. The girls often spoke at the same time, or one on the other's behalf. Persephone had never known any twins before, and she found Anne and Elizabeth utterly endearing.

She was also grateful for the distraction they caused their uncle, who turned the appealing force of his attention to them instead, allowing Persephone a moment to collect herself.

Why was he here? It had been a mere day since she had watched him slip from her chamber, clad in his rumpled trousers and coat. She had discovered his cravat protruding from beneath her bed after he had gone. She could not say why, but the sudden, shameful urge to bring the scrap of linen to her nose to catch a trace of him had overtaken her. Shaving soap and Rafe Sutton and...why, if sin possessed a scent, it would surely be the same.

She had frantically tucked it beneath her pillow, where it still remained.

He was wearing a fresh neck cloth now, this one tied expertly and plainly. No ostentatious waterfalls for him. Quite unlike Cousin Bartholomew, who dressed as excessively as he drank. The contrast between Rafe Sutton and Bartholomew could not be more apparent. Rafe was all lean, sinewy grace. He was handsome and he knew it. Bartholomew, meanwhile, was...none of those things.

"Did you come to see Miss Wren?" Anne asked her uncle then, bringing a mortified flush to Persephone's cheeks.

Children, she had learned, were not very adept at hiding their opinions or learning when to hold their tongues. But then, neither were adults in many circumstances.

He glanced in her direction, a slow grin curving his lips. "It is always a pleasure to see Miss Wren, of course. However, I came to see your papa. I needed to discuss something with him."

Their audience would have been business related, Persephone supposed. Her employer and his family owned a well-known gaming hell called The Sinner's Palace. How ridiculous it was, the lump of disappointment settling in her belly. Why had the silly rambling of children filled her with a false, ludicrous sense of hope? Indeed, why would he have come here to seek *her* out? And furthermore, why should she want him to?

The answers swirled through her mind, damning as any accusation.

You find him handsome, Persephone. And that is dangerous. Men in general are not to be trusted, but most particularly never rogues from the East End who swagger when they walk and have a face that would make even the most hardened of ladies sigh in appreciation.

Yes, there was that. But also, it was foolish how weak she was, even after the years she had spent at the mercy of Cousin Bartholomew's selfish whims. The realization she could be so moved by Rafe Sutton, whom she had frantically drugged with laudanum two nights before, was humbling indeed.

It was not his looks—pleasing though they were—which drew her to him. It was the way he smiled, the way he moved. It was *everything* about him. And that was very much a problem.

"Miss Wren?"

Oh, curse it. She had not been attending the conversation, and now Mr. Rafe Sutton was looking at her expectantly, as if he had asked her a question of great import. A question she had not heard since she had been far too busy musing on his irresistible male qualities.

Her face felt as if it were aflame. Thanks to her hair, it likely was. *An unfortunate coloring,* Cousin Bartholomew had remarked once. *I never did care for redheads. They're always spotted and pink-faced. However, I suppose you shall have to do.*

"Yes, Mr. Sutton?" She forced a benign smile to her lips.

"We are in agreement, then," he said, grinning so deeply, his dimples appeared.

Her stupid heart was beating faster again. Perhaps there was something grievously wrong with her. That was the only satisfactory explanation.

"Forgive me, sir. I do not know what you are saying we have agreed upon," she admitted, omitting the reason.

It would hardly do to admit the man had somehow absconded with all her wits when he had left her room. But clearly, he had. Nothing else made sense. He was a thief. A handsome and a tempting one.

He winked. "That these two girls are not fast runners. Not at all. Quite slow, they are. Slower than a pair of little moles."

He had winked at her. The audacity! And why was he here in the gardens anyway? He had come to speak to her employer, and now he was lingering in the same space where she had to be. The girls were in her care. She did not dare let them from her sight, for she had already realized they were quite...*adventurous*. Yes, that was a nice, proper word to describe the rather unusual exuberance and curiosity of Miss Anne and Miss Elizabeth.

"Young ladies do not run, Mr. Sutton," she reminded him, despite her determination to avoid chastising them for the very same action before his unexpected arrival.

She sounded far too much like her own dreaded governesses.

A succession of them, in short order.

No one can govern this horrible chit, one governess had said when she left.

Cousin Bartholomew had agreed. And then he had promptly found a governess more adept at killing souls and crushing spirits than the last.

"I cannot believe it." Rafe Sutton was shaking his head slowly, hands planted rudely on his hips.

Staring at her.

Making her feel even hotter. Surely she ought to be cold. Chilled to the bone. The air was cool today. She did not have a wrap. And yet, she felt quite overheated. As if it were a summer's day.

"What can you not believe, Mr. Sutton?" she dared to ask, only because the twins were watching her with wide, curious eyes.

She was meant to be an example. To be polite and calm and proper in all circumstances. Increasingly difficult with this troublesome man about.

He was naked in my bed.

No!

Cease this manner of thought at once, Persephone.

"I cannot believe that you would believe such nonsense," he elaborated. "Of course all ladies can and do run. However, the question is whether or not Anne and Elizabeth are quick enough—"

"We are!" Elizabeth shouted, jumping twice in her exuberance.

"You see, Miss Wren?" Mr. Sutton's eyes remained fixed upon her, much to her unease. "Anne thinks she is quite speedy."

"Elizabeth," Persephone and her charges corrected simultaneously.

Mr. Sutton laughed, turning his attention back to his nieces. "Forgive me."

"We love you, Uncle Rafe!" Anne announced. "Even if you cannot tell us apart, you are one of our favoritest uncles."

"Favorite, girls," Persephone felt obliged to correct. "*Favoritest* is not a word."

"Ought to be," he commented. "I'm deuced proud to be a favoritest uncle."

"We love Uncle Hart and Uncle Damian and Uncle Wolf, too," Elizabeth said.

"There's the way to make a cove feel special."

"You are special!" decreed one twin.

"Wonderfully so," agreed the other.

"If only your enthusiasm for my charms were extended to Miss Wren," he said to the girls before casting another glance in Persephone's direction.

She would not willingly divulge enthusiasm of any sort for his *charms*. To her shame, she could likely list each one. However, she had no place taking notice. This was her life now. She was a governess. She *had* to be a governess, at least until she no longer required a guardian to decide what she did with her funds. And even then, she shuddered to think what would happen should she emerge from hiding.

She forced herself back to the present, where a handsome, quick-to-smile scoundrel was awaiting her answer. "I am enthusiastic about a great many things, Mr. Sutton. The progress Anne and Elizabeth are making with their reading, for instance. Your dubious charms, however, are not among them."

His lips twitched, almost as if he found amusement in her less-than-subtle reprimand. "'Tis a shame. I have many to offer."

And she had seen more than her fair share of them.

"Mr. Sutton, this conversation is quite improper," she told him coolly.

Although it was not done to reprimand her employer's family member, there was something about Rafe Sutton that ruffled every last one of her feathers.

"What's unproper?" Anne asked, sounding curious.

Oh dear.

It would not do for the children to run to their parents with tales of the new governess telling their beloved Uncle Rafe he had been *unproper*. She had only just secured this position. Finding herself settled and in a good situation such as this one had been an impossible feat until now.

"Never mind that, you thimble full of trouble," he told Anne, the easy tenderness in his voice chipping away at the block of ice that had formed around Persephone's heart. "I still do not believe you are quick enough to run about the gardens fifteen times each before my pocket watch tells me it is half past two in the afternoon. Neither you, nor your sister."

"We are," the girls declared simultaneously.

Mr. Sutton sighed. "I do not think you ought to dare try."

He spoke so smoothly that one could almost confuse him for a true gentleman. The son of a duke or earl.

Almost.

Here and there, his accent slipped. When he had been deep in his cups and under the influence of the laudanum she had secreted in his glass, he had lost quite a bit of his polish, his East End origins showing.

The girls jumped up and down. "We must try! We must!

Persephone compressed her lips to keep from smiling. Curse him, he *was* charming. He seemed to know just what to say to prompt a response in Anne and Elizabeth.

"Off you go, then," he said with a benevolent wave of his hand.

He did not need to offer further encouragement. The twins raced away, grasping fistfuls of their skirts and laughing. Persephone watched them go with a grudging sense of admiration for Rafe Sutton's subtle skills with children. Perhaps she could employ the same tactic to persuade the girls to practice their needlepoint.

"That was quite clever of you," she said, turning back to him only to find he had moved.

He was nearer now, bringing with him all the intensity of the magnetism he exuded. And his scent on the breeze, ruffling the hair at her temple, poorly trapped by her bonnet.

He was grinning as well, those dimples taunting her. "Thank you. I fancy myself reasonably clever on occasion. Not clever enough the night before last, 'owever."

There it was, the hint of his true background slipping through like sunlight in the cracks of closed curtains. Along with the reminder of what had transpired. She had deliberately evaded his questions.

She should have known he would not have simply allowed the matter to slip away. "I am afraid I do not know what you are speaking of, sir."

That was a lie. She had been doing rather a lot of that since she had run from Cousin Bartholomew's odious clutches. And she expected to continue to do so until...well, for as long as necessary.

"The knot on my knowledge box, Miss Wren," he elaborated.

Oh. He was concerned about the knock he had taken to the head?

"You injured yourself," she supplied, turning her gaze back to the gardens, where her charges were currently running rampant.

"One!" the girls cried as they completed their first tour and continued on.

"Injured myself," he repeated, his tone suggesting he did not believe her.

"Yes." *Remain calm, Persephone. Above all, be polite.*

"How?"

I gave you too much laudanum, and you pitched headlong into a table.

"You were a trifle disguised that evening," she said calmly, still avoiding his gaze. "It is to be understood, of course, given the events of that day, poor Lady Octavia having been attacked... You need not worry. I shall not judge you or carry a tale, and I trust you will return the favor."

Heavens, if he told her employers he had been naked in her bed, she would be gone in the blink of an eye. As damning as the loss of her position would be, the damage such a tale would inflict upon all future situations would be nearly irreparable.

"That ain't an explanation, my dear."

He had moved closer. His voice was nearly at her ear, the low baritone an undeniably pleasant sound. She turned toward him at last.

"Two," called one of the girls as the sound of small feet running returned.

Thirteen more rounds? Surely Persephone would perish of mortification first.

Or longing.

The unwanted thought lingered as she studied Rafe Sutton's handsome countenance for any hint he knew what she had done. "What do you recall, Mr. Sutton? Perhaps we should begin there."

She was blustering. Delaying. But she could not bear for him to continue prodding her in this fashion. What if he remembered something? Slipping the laudanum into his brandy had been foolish and dangerous. If her employer were to learn she had drugged his brother, the consequences would prove dire, she had no doubt.

She shivered, for whilst Mr. Jasper Sutton was a benevolent man, he was also fiercely protective of his family. And if he dismissed her, where would she go? Falsifying another letter to recommend her for a future placement would be reckless, and she needed more time.

"Did you knock me on the idea pot?" he asked, stroking his jaw.

There was a slight hint of golden whiskers on that strong angle, as if he had not shaved that morning. For a reason she did not dare investigate, she found herself wondering at the texture. If she ran her fingertips over it, would it feel prickly to the touch?

"Of course I did not assault your person, Mr. Sutton," she answered.

"Four," announced Elizabeth, sounding a bit breathless from her exertion.

Four? Goodness, had Persephone been so caught up in Rafe Sutton that she had missed the third circumnavigation, or had Elizabeth made an error in her counting?

"Then how did I end up with an aching nob?"

"Must we discuss this?" she hissed, taking a step to her right, putting more distance between herself and his maddening presence.

But Mr. Sutton merely followed her, determined to have the answers she had no wish to give. "Yes, we must."

Rafe studied Miss Wren closely, wondering why the devil she was being so stubborn. Could she not see that he needed answers? That a man could not wake in a woman's bed bare-arsed naked, without a bloody inkling of what had occurred the night before, and not have questions?

"Why should it matter so much to you?" she asked, frowning at him in her stern, governess way that made him want to kiss her.

What was it about this wench that made her so comely?

"Five," Anne declared, running by.

His attempt to distract the twins had worked

marvelously. He had the opportunity to speak with Miss Wren alone. And yet, she remained as slippery as ever.

He did not want to force her answer, but she was making it impossible.

"Because it matters," he responded, being equally evasive in his reply. "Tell me, or I will find it necessary to speak with my brother about that night."

She went pale, the lovely flush fading from her delicate cheekbones, and he regretted his words. But it was too late to recall them.

Miss Wren glanced away. "You fell into a table as you were disrobing. That is how you struck your head, Mr. Sutton."

What did not make sense to Rafe, and what had been troubling him ever since he had risen to find himself in her bed, was how the floating hell he had managed to get so thoroughly sotted from brandy. He had not a single memory of drinking to excess that evening. Only the brandy, then a swirling feeling, as if his head were too light for his body. The brandy had been oddly bitter...

"There was something wrong with that bloody brandy," he grumbled. "There had to 'ave been."

But what? And how?

For the first time, a rather sinister thought rose in his mind. Now that it had taken up residence there, he was not sure why the possibility had not occurred to him sooner.

"The brandy was drugged," he said, making the realization aloud.

At his side, Miss Wren had stiffened. "Why should you think so?"

It was the only explanation for his complete lack of recollection. Rafe was no swill tub, though he was hardly a stranger to the drink. "Because I can't recall a single damned moment beyond brandy and you."

Had he kissed her that night? Not to have taken those lush lips with his would have been a sin. Rafe would have sworn kissing her was an experience he would not forget, regardless of how soused he had been.

It was difficult indeed to imagine this prim woman welcoming him into her bed. She was so bleeding icy. And despite her undeniable beauty, she was also the last sort of female he would have tumbled. He had never been stirred by ladies with precise well-bred accents and manners. Lusty, knowledgeable widows were his standard fare.

"Six!" Anne cried, her cheeks rosy, her dark hair flying wildly behind her.

The girls looked as if they were losing some of their vigor, which meant he needed to conduct this conversation with haste before his curious nieces would interrupt.

"What was my behavior like?" he asked their governess.

"It is far better for it to remain unmentioned."

"Hmm." He leaned nearer, realizing his mistake as he did so. Miss Wren smelled bloody delectable. Winter's soap, unless he missed his guess, all flowers and sunshine and everything the East End was not. "Did I touch you, Miss Wren?"

Because if he had not, and she had been willing that night, by God, he was a bigger fool than he had believed.

"Not in the manner you are suggesting," she said, keeping her gaze averted, as if watching a pair of children racing wildly about a small London garden were the most riveting of sights.

"Seven!"

"And what manner am I suggesting?" he could not resist prodding, hoping to watch the color rise to her creamy skin once more.

Scarcely any of it was visible—not enough. He would

dearly love to unwrap her himself. Pity she was the twins'
governess. She would have made a wonderful challenge.

"The lascivious manner, sir." She turned toward him, and
he noted the remarkable striations in her eyes. Flecks of gold
ornamented the wide discs of her pupils. "Do not think to
play your seducer's games with me, Mr. Sutton. I have no
wish for trouble."

"But you have already found a great lot of it, have you
not?" He rubbed his jaw, considering her. "All that mayhem
with Lady Octavia must have left you ill at ease. And then
what happened between us…"

Which remained a mystery on his part.

"Perhaps we should agree never to speak of that awful
night again," she suggested coolly.

"Eight!"

Blast. The girls were over halfway through their paces.

"There is one thing I cannot understand, Miss Wren. Who
would have drugged Jasper's bingo, and why?"

"Bingo?" She blinked, her lashes glinting with gold in the
afternoon light.

"Brandy," he explained.

This conundrum had him so flummoxed that he had
failed to suppress the cant from his speech. Or perhaps it was
not the conundrum, but rather, the woman.

"Surely you had partaken before your arrival," she said.

A sudden memory hit him, of pacing up and down the
thick woolen carpets, the brandy abandoned atop a table at
his back. He had turned, worried over his sister-in-law, who
had been slashed by a blade, and there had been Miss Wren,
hovering near his glass. She had moved swiftly, away from it.

"You," he said, stunned.

"What of me?" she asked, her tone as calm as ever.

But he did not miss her sudden pallor.

"You are the one who drugged me, Miss Wren," he said,

knowing it was true when he spied the flash of fear in her gaze.

But he still had no notion *why*.

Why would this proper, elegant governess he had only met for the first time two days ago have drugged his brandy? What possible purpose had it served?

"Eleven!" Elizabeth's triumphant call severed the moment.

Rafe discovered he had been so absorbed in his dialogue with Miss Wren that he had failed to hear the girls call out *nine* and *ten*.

"That is quite enough locomotion, Anne and Elizabeth!" The governess returned her attention to his nieces swiftly, the snap of authority ringing in her voice. "We must return to our lessons."

"But we haven't reached fifteen," Anne said, pouting.

What the devil?

Miss Wren was hurrying away from him now, moving toward the garden and the girls. He followed in her wake, confusion and anger swirling and fogging up his mind. The cunning wench had drugged him. And now she was fleeing as if she were a thief who had been caught pilfering the silver. Just who was Miss Wren, anyway?

"We have not finished our discussion," he warned grimly.

"Yes we have." She cast a glance at him over her shoulder, and he did not miss the fear in her expression. "You are playing a dangerous game, and I want no part of it, Mr. Sutton. I need this position, and I shall not allow you to ruin it with your spurious delusions."

Spurious delusions indeed.

The wench was dicked in the nob, and she was looking after his nieces.

He was going to have to tell Jasper about this.

But how?

CHAPTER 4

*P*ersephone passed the days following Rafe Sutton's garden visit and subsequent accusations in a state of tense anticipation. Each time she spoke to Mr. Jasper Sutton or Lady Octavia, she expected to hear the damning words telling her she would need to find another situation. That she would be relieved of her position without a written character to recommend her as she struggled to find yet another post.

You slipped laudanum into my brother-in-law's brandy, she imagined Lady Octavia saying, her voice stern and cold as ice. *How dare you betray our family? Leave this house immediately and never return.*

Instead, Lady Octavia had praised her over the progress Anne and Elizabeth were making with their letters. No one in the household had seen her alone with Rafe that night or morning as the house had been bustling with frantic activity. Her secret was safe.

But for how long?

That was the question that haunted her even as she walked toward the waiting carriage. This afternoon, she was off to a bookseller where she would seek new reading material for her charges. Ordinarily, she preferred to travel in public infrequently, lest she be seen by someone who might carry word back to Cousin Bartholomew. However, she was wound as tightly as a watch spring, anticipating Rafe Sutton's blow to her carefully constructed peace at any moment. The twins were in need of more challenging books, and Lady Octavia had offered the use of the carriage and the accompaniment of a groom on her excursion. And leaving the confines of the town house would do wonders to help shake the worries and fears haunting her.

At least, she hoped it would.

A groom opened the carriage door for her, and she stepped up and inside, her mind so filled with thoughts that she failed to realize the conveyance was not empty until she was nearly within.

There, seated in the shadows of the bench to her left, sat Rafe Sutton, long legs crossed at the ankle in an indolent pose. His boots were gleaming, his trousers the perfect complement to his dark, well-cut coat. The hat pulled low over his brow did nothing to diminish the appearance of those blond curls. He looked like a fallen angel come to claim the wicked.

Her heart felt as if it had dropped through her stomach.

"Mr. Sutton!" she said on a shocked gasp, freezing on the step.

"Get in," he ordered her, his voice low and commanding.

The easy flirtation was gone from his mannerism. The charming rogue blessed with dimples who had dared to wink at her was nowhere to be seen.

"What are you doing in this carriage?" she demanded, ignoring his curt directive.

"Come in, and you shall see." His voice was calm and smooth and yet, there was an underlying hardness to it, the suggestion that he would not accept any outcome other than the one he wished.

"Why should I?" She cast a glance over her shoulder, trying to find the groom who had opened the door and seeing no one.

"You need not worry about young Jonas," Mr. Sutton said smoothly. "I have greased his hand quite generously."

He had bribed the servant?

Her heart stuttered and tripped over itself. "What do you want, sir?"

"You know what I want," he said, his hazel stare traveling down her body in a thorough sweep that left her skin tingling. "Now step inside like a good governess."

Surely he was not suggesting he wanted something *amorous* in nature from her. But then, he would hardly be the first. She supposed nothing should surprise her. Her four-and-twenty years may as well have been a lifetime for the experiences she had endured.

And yet despite that... Oh! What is the matter with you, Persephone?

Why did the threat of an impending ride in a carriage with Rafe Sutton make heat blossom in her belly and spread lower, to a far more forbidden place? Why did her body react to his, trusting him in a way her mind did not dare?

Barraged by a rush of confusing emotions—trepidation, longing, curiosity—she hesitated, chastising herself inwardly.

"Get in, or I will pay a call to my brother this very moment," he added.

Persephone stepped up and into the vehicle, settling herself on the seat opposite his. The carriage door closed with a loud snap. Mr. Sutton rapped on the roof, and it rocked into motion.

He had planned this, she realized. How efficiently and effortlessly he was spiriting her away. She ought to be alarmed, and yet, there was something about this man that felt somehow, inherently, different from the other, far more unscrupulous men she had known.

This man had teased and flirted and was wonderfully sweet to his nieces. Even when he had arisen in her bed, he had never attempted to press his suit.

"Where are you taking me?" she asked him.

He raised a brow. "I'll be the one asking the questions, Miss Wren. Not you."

She swallowed a lump of uncertainty. "You do realize my employers will wonder if I fail to return, do you not, sir?"

He cocked his head, considering her with a vibrant regard that made her long to shift on her seat. His hands, large and gloved like a proper gentleman's, rested on his thighs. The fingers of the right lightly drummed against his trousers. She wished he were not wearing a hat, for it seemed a shame for his golden hair to be confined beneath the brim.

"And you do realize, Miss Wren, that you drugged the brother of your employer with laudanum, stripped him of his clothes, beat him over the head, and spent the night in the same bed as him?" he returned, his tone mild.

She could not suppress her wince at his description of the unfortunate circumstances which had seemed to yoke them. "I did none of those things, sir, and while I must apologize for allowing you to sleep off the ill effects of your brandy drinking in my room, I had no choice."

Well, that was not true at all, was it? She *had* drugged him, and she *had* spent the night in the same bed as well. Her lie was growing weary, as was she. How to extricate herself from this mess she had created with her own reckless panic?

"No choice but to lie there in bed with me all night long, knowing there was nary a stitch to cover my bare arse beneath the counterpane?" he asked.

He was speaking with the accent of a gentleman once

more. Aside from the subject matter of his discourse, there was not a hint of the East End in his perfect speech. It was almost as if there were two different Rafe Suttons. Which one of them was real? She could not be sure.

"I did not peek, sir, if your modesty is what concerns you," she offered, attempting to deflect the subject.

"It ain't what concerns me at all. Your motivations do, however." He paused, his expression growing stern. "Why did you do what you did, Miss Wren?"

Why indeed? Her reasoning in the moment had been abrupt.

She was thinking of her past when she blurted her next question. "Do you believe yourself the first gentleman to force his attentions upon a servant?"

Persephone regretted her choice of words the moment the query left her, for she did not mean to suggest *he* had forced himself on her. Merely that her experience had left her with a tremendous distrust of handsome rogues who attempted to seduce the governess. One of them had not accepted her refusal. It had not been him, but another.

And Rafe Sutton had paid the price. Guilt skewered her. She had never intended to do him harm. What Lord Gregson had done to her had made Persephone suspicious of every man, and she had reacted with reckless haste.

Mr. Sutton's jaw went rigid. "What are you suggesting, Miss Wren?"

His voice was silken and yet laden with an inherent hint of menace.

How to explain the sudden fear that had overtaken her, the worry which had been shadowing her every interaction since she had abandoned her previous post? She could tell him, could she not, without mentioning any other details? Surely admitting she was a governess who had been importuned by the eldest son of her former employer was not tantamount to telling him who she truly was and what she had escaped from first.

It was apparent he believed she was accusing him of forcing himself upon her, and that was not what she had meant at all. Her words, like her thoughts, were a jumbled hodgepodge of pure confusion.

Time for the truth.

She took a deep, fortifying breath. "I was not referring to you, Mr. Sutton. I am attempting to explain my actions that night. You were charming and handsome and you were flirting. I...I panicked because of a former, regrettable circumstance. Pray forgive me. You are correct. I *did* slip laudanum into your brandy when your back was turned. But only out of an instinctive need to protect myself. I did not mean to pour as much into the brandy as I did."

The silence, when she had completed the swift rush of her confession, was almost deafening, broken by nothing other than the steady rhythm of plodding hooves and the jangle of tack and other street sounds. Mr. Sutton was watching her intently, his expression unreadable. His jaw was clenched, his hazel eyes dark.

How she wished again for the easy, joking mannerism of his arrival at the garden when he had teased his nieces into running about like hoydens. The man opposite her now seemed dangerous, his face all sharp angles and planes.

"You admit to drugging me?" he asked at last.

She inhaled, not realizing she had been holding her breath until that very moment. "Yes. But I did so in fear. I regretted my actions at once."

"You needn't fear me, Miss Wren. Not now. Not ever. Rafe Sutton doesn't need to steal a woman's virtue. She gives it to 'im freely."

His low rasp curled around her, wrapping her in warmth and an inexplicable longing. He was not the same sort of man as Lord Gregson. Whilst her initial interaction with him that mad night had led her to react with a frenzied terror, the rational part of her mind could discern the difference. Not every man was a predator.

Only some.

"There are men who prey upon women for reasons other than a lack of charm," she said quietly, thinking of Lord Gregson.

Hateful thought.

Yet, necessary.

He had been handsome as well, though his looks were diminished in her memory now by his villainous deeds. She had no doubt he could have had his choice of demi-mondaines or diamonds of the first water. However, he was the sort of man who thrived on power. Specifically, his over others. And that was a different beast entirely. It was a beast she knew well enough, thanks to Cousin Bartholomew

"I 'm not such a man," he said.

She did not doubt Rafe Sutton wielded his charm as if it were a weapon. Between his undeniable good looks and the magnetism of his presence, he could likely woo even the most devout devotee of propriety.

"Nonetheless, I could not be certain of that at the time," she managed primly.

"And so you took matters into your own hands. *A former, regrettable circumstance*, you said. What happened?"

There was a hint of menace in his voice, and she could not be certain whom it was directed toward. Persephone shifted, dreadfully uncomfortable in the confines of this carriage, not knowing where he was taking her or why.

Speaking of Lord Gregson was not a particularly easy feat, either.

She inhaled slowly, collecting herself for fear the terror would return, clogging her throat. "My previous situation involved a gentleman who believed it was his right to do whatever he wished with the governess of his younger sisters."

Her position in the Earl of Landsdowne's household had been one of many unhappy tenures as governess over the years she had spent running from her cousin. However, it was burned upon her memory for a reason aside from her displeasure.

"Whatever he wished." Mr. Sutton's voice was cutting now. "He forced himself upon you?"

Persephone swallowed that rising sense of panic, never far whenever she thought of what had happened in her small room that evening. "He attempted to do so."

His nostrils flared, his hands clenching into fists—the only two movements he made. He might have been fashioned of stone save for the sound of his voice. "Who?"

"Viscount Gregson."

Just saying his name made the bitter taste of bile rise in the back of her throat. He was a despicable, vile scoundrel. Little wonder the governesses before her had fled their posts.

"Lord Gregson," Mr. Sutton repeated. "Tall cull, with dark hair? Eldest son of the Earl of Landsdowne, yes?"

She had not supposed Rafe Sutton would be familiar with Lord Gregson. Her blood went cold, panic setting in. Surely they were not friends? Her heart was pounding faster, her mouth going dry.

"I was hired as the governess to Lord Landsdowne's younger daughters," she acknowledged. "Whenever he was in residence, he made certain to make advances, which I ignored. But he refused to accept my denial. One night, I woke to find him in my room. I was attempting to fight him off when my cries alerted some of the other members of the household, and he mercifully stopped. His body was so heavy atop mine, pinning me to the mattress. I remember his breath, hot and smelling of sour wine. I was trying to get away, but he would not allow it. He was stronger than I was, and he kept telling me I was a forward chit, that he knew I wanted him..."

The words trailed off as emotion overwhelmed her.

She gagged.

In a swift flurry of graceful movement, Rafe sat beside her on the bench, his hand on the small of her back in a gesture of comfort. "Are you going to cast up your accounts?"

Mayhap. She could not speak at the moment. She was remembering Lord Gregson's breath, the sweat dripping off his brow, the clammy hand clamped over her mouth. How difficult it had been to breathe, to scream. She had bitten him as hard as she could, and the taste of his blood, coppery and strange, had filled her mouth.

Repulsive.

His hands had been everywhere. And he had told her to keep still, to be quiet.

Cease moving. You want this. You know it as well as I.

But she had not wanted him. Nor had she encouraged any of his many advances. His excuses to find reasons to be near her had been troubling. The night she had arisen to his presence in the darkness of her room had been utterly terrifying.

"Deep breaths, Miss Wren," Mr. Sutton was urging her now, jolting her from the violence of her recollections to the present.

The carriage was still swaying over bumpy Mayfair roads. His hand passed up and down her spine in slow, steady strokes. She obeyed, dragging air into her lungs, and with it his masculine scent. Time to tamp down the memories. To force them into the box in the dark corners of her mind.

"I spent the rest of that night hiding in the library. In the morning, I gathered my belongings and I left."

"Slow and steady now," he said, his voice gentling,

becoming almost tender. "Lord Gregson ain't here. He can't 'urt you."

Mr. Sutton was losing some of his polish. The *h* had vanished once more. He was upset, she realized. On her behalf.

When all she had done thus far was pour laudanum into his brandy and lie to him.

A rush of shame made her cheeks go hot. She had done nothing to deserve his sympathy.

"I am sorry," she managed. "I should not have assumed you would be the same. When I realized I had poured too much into your brandy, I did not know what to do. I need this post quite desperately. I cannot afford to have to secure another, so I took you to my chamber, fearing Mr. Sutton would see the state you were in and guess at what I had done. I needed to hide you until the effects had worn off, and I was desperately hoping you would not remember what had happened."

Except, she had not planned on him being so stubbornly determined to wrest the truth from her.

Miraculously, his slow, steady caress up and down her back continued, in spite of her revelations. "When did you knock me on the knowledge box?"

"I did not hit you," she hastened to explain, wincing as she recalled the sickening thud of his head hitting her bedside table. "You were removing your clothes because you wished to sleep, and I could not persuade you against the wisdom of disrobing regardless of how hard I tried. You lost your balance, striking your head on a piece of furniture as you fell."

"Little wonder it still hurts like the bleeding devil."

She had no doubt it would. "The blow was strong enough to knock you insensate for a few moments. I had to watch over you, so I managed to help you into the bed, and there you remained for the night. I did not dare risk sleeping anywhere else for fear of discovery."

"That explains the wall of pillows you built."

"I had to be certain there was a boundary."

"You trusted me enough to sleep at my side the entire night?"

"I had no choice," she admitted. "But I realized, too late of course, and only after I had poured the laudanum into your glass, that I was allowing my fear of what had happened before to inform my judgment. You had given me no reason to suspect you would force yourself upon me. I simply... I panicked."

"You were attacked by that vile swine. It is understandable that you would not soon trust another man."

His calm understanding was almost more than she could bear. "You are being kind to me. Why?"

"I'm a kind chap." His easy grin returned.

Something in her heart shifted. Slid into place. How she wished she were someone else, and that she could simply revel in this man's charm.

But she could not fall beneath the easy spell of a man like Rafe Sutton.

Just two more months, Persephone, she reminded herself. When she turned five-and-twenty, Cousin Bartholomew could no longer be a threat to her inheritance. Still, her birthday seemed a lifetime away.

"I do not deserve your kindness." The words escaped her, the closest she dared come to a complete confession.

The truth was, she was continuing to deceive him, just as she was deceiving Mr. Jasper Sutton and Lady Octavia. Her currency had become lies and manipulation. Anything to protect herself. She was little better than Cousin Bartholomew.

"Everyone in this mad world of ours deserves some kindness and understanding, Miss Wren," Rafe Sutton said, his hand stilling on her back at last. "With the exception of bloody Lord Gregson. That bastard deserves what is coming to 'im."

The menace had returned to his words, as had the stiffness to his bearing. She shivered, and it was not entirely from the cold. "What do you mean, Mr. Sutton?"

Surely he did not intend to exact vengeance upon Lord Gregson on her behalf.

Did he?

His response was a grim smile. "You needn't worry, my dear." With that, he rapped on the carriage roof thrice, and the vehicle slowed before coming to a halt. "Good day, Miss Wren. I'll take my leave."

The carriage door opened, sending in the sunlight and a burst of cool air, along with the undiluted noise of the street.

He rose from the bench, then descended from the vehicle in one fluid motion, all lean strength as he leapt to the street below. When his boots planted on terra firma, he turned to give her a tip of his hat.

And then he simply walked away.

The door closed, the carriage lumbering on.

How empty and quiet the vehicle had suddenly become, bereft of his magnificent presence. Persephone did her utmost to banish the unwanted longing echoing through her. But it was burning to life like a fire too long starved of air, and she very much feared that if she was not able to control this inconvenient attraction she had to Mr. Rafe Sutton, she would end up getting burned.

CHAPTER 5

*H*aving been born to the rookeries had its benefits. One of them was learning how to hide in plain sight. How to blend with the shadows and await one's prey. In his youth, Rafe had been a dab hand at pickpocketing fancy culls who wandered about like fat hens in a fox's den. He had learned many lessons in those rough days before The Sinner's Palace had become one of the most sought-after gaming hells in London. And one of those lessons was about to suit him well.

The best time to strike was when a man was drunk, when he had recently drained his ballocks, or when he thought he was about to accomplish both or either of those pleasantly sated states. He had already used this time-honored tenet to have a mildly violent discussion with Lord Aidan Weir concerning his sister Pen. He was about to have another with Viscount Gregson on behalf of a different woman.

It had taken him only a few days to learn the habits of his quarry. And so it was that he found himself waiting to enter an adjoining chamber at The Garden of Flora. His presence this evening was not, as it had been on previous occasions, to take pleasure. But rather, to confer pain and humiliation.

Madame Laurent had been kind enough, when he had relayed his information concerning Lord Gregson, to offer her assistance. As the owner of one of the finer, if more depraved, establishments catering to the lusty whims of London, Sophie did not tolerate any patrons with abusive tendencies.

The greatest asset of an abbess was her ladies, and if her ladies were injured or worse, it affected her purse. Sophie understood the health and well-being of the women in her employ was distinctly connected to how much coin she could collect from her patrons. If a man were to mistreat any of them, or if he were found to have passed on the Covent Garden ague, he was prohibited from returning.

If a cull is willing to force himself on an innocent governess in his family's home, Christ knows what he is capable of, Rafe had told Sophie.

Being an intelligent and shrewd businesswoman, she had agreed, promising to send word the next time Lord Gregson arrived at The Garden of Flora. She had also agreed to set up a tableau rendering Rafe's plan far more easily enacted. Tonight was the night.

Lord Gregson was about to have the basting of his spoiled, lordly life.

The door to the chamber opened, and a brunette named Mignonette emerged. In truth, her name was likely Mary or Sarah, or something equally plain. Sophie required all her ladies to take the names of flowers.

Mignonette was one of the most expensive ladies at The Garden of Flora for a very good reason. She stopped at nothing to please whomever was fortunate enough to enjoy her company for the evening. Strangely, however, her lush beauty, on display in a diaphanous dressing gown, did not stir him this evening.

All his thoughts were for a sunset-haired governess who had drugged him and dragged him into her bed. It made no sense, and yet, there was something about prim Miss Wren that brought out all the possessive instincts he had. Not just desire but a deeper, stronger connection. A bond he could neither explain nor define.

And that was why he found himself here, waiting to mete out justice to that slimy arsehole Lord Gregson, on her behalf. If ever he had known of a man who needed to be beaten to death with a sack of his own shite, it was he. Rafe's blood ran hot with impotent fury as he remembered how pale and shaken Miss Wren had been in the carriage as she had confessed to what had occurred at her previous post. She had come perilously close to retching. The reminder sent a resurgence of bloodlust slamming through him.

"His lordship is awaiting his surprise," Mignonette said softly, extending her arm to offer him a rather wicked-looking cat-o'-nine-tails.

Apparently, some patrons of The Garden of Flora enjoyed being flogged. Lord Gregson was one of them. That salient bit of information had given Rafe all the ammunition he required.

He took the whip from Mignonette, surprised by the heft of it in his hand. "Thank you, darling."

Mignonette came nearer, bringing with her the rich scent of her perfume, which was not nearly as pleasing as the floral notes of Miss Wren's Winter's soap. "Of course. I had not realized how despicable Lord Gregson is. We thank you for rooting out a viper on our behalf."

Mignonette's accent suggested she had been raised by the quality. She spoke with an eloquence that was difficult to feign. Quite a bit like Miss Wren.

He inclined his head, his fingers tightening on the braided leather hilt of the whip. "My pleasure."

"Perhaps I can see to your pleasure later," she suggested, running a finger lightly down his forearm.

Still, he felt nothing. Not a hint of interest. Nor a stirring of his cock. He told himself his lack of response was because of the fury igniting his veins.

"Some other night, love," he said softly, giving her a smile he knew the ladies always adored.

Women and dimples. He'd never understand the fascination, but he most assuredly wasn't against exploiting it for his own benefit.

She pouted. "If you insist."

"I'm afraid I do." He had other matters to attend to, far more important ones.

Rafe took his leave of the lovely Mignonette and ventured into the adjoining chamber where Lord Gregson anticipated his "surprise." Madame Laurent had a host of devices and pieces of furniture which lent themselves to the particular vices of her guests. In this instance, Lord Gregson was strapped to a narrow, padded bench, lying prone, a blindfold tied over his eyes. His wrists were bound above his head, and his ankles were held in place with buckled straps at the opposite end. The sight of his pale arse made Rafe ill. At least the bastard was facedown.

"What took you so long, Mignonette?" the viscount asked, having no notion of what he was about to endure.

But then, it was only fitting, for neither had Miss Wren. She had been innocently sleeping when this detestable scoundrel had attempted to force himself upon her. Rafe could only imagine the fear which must have gripped her. Witnessing her reaction to the memories of that night in the carriage haunted him still.

Drove him here.

Now.

To this moment of vengeance.

"Forgive me for the delay," he drawled, striding forward, preparing to strike.

"What the bloody deuce?"

Lord Gregson's alarm was as apparent as it was enjoyable. He instantly struggled with his bonds, fear lacing his words.

"You cannot escape, you piece of horse shite," Rafe said, unable to keep the note of savage satisfaction from his own voice. "Rather similar, ain't it?"

"Similar to what? What the devil is happening? Who are you, and where is Mignonette?" demanded Lord Gregson, panicked now as he tugged wildly at his wrists and ankles, to no avail.

"Similar to the way you attempted to force yourself on an innocent governess." He tested the whip, cracking it against the carpets. "You do recall, do you not? Stealing your way into her room in the night, forcing yourself into her bed, pinning her down and telling her she *wanted* you to violate her? Ignoring her when she told you to stop?"

Rafe had to pause and clench his jaw, his rage overflowing like the swelling banks of a flooded river.

"I never violated anyone!" Lord Gregson denied, his voice high-pitched with fear. "What are you going to do to me?"

"You never violated her, because she was able to fight your drunken arse off and alert the household," he bit out. "As for what I'm going to do to you, Lord Gregson, that's simple. I'm going to exact retribution."

"Please, no," Lord Gregson whimpered.

"This one is for Miss Wren," Rafe said grimly, drawing back the cat-o'-nine-tails and striking with all his might.

The lordling screamed in pain. Rafe did not so much as flinch as he drew back the whip again, undaunted by the red welts marring Lord Gregson's back and hairy arse.

"And this is for any other innocents you may have defiled."

The whip cracked again.

"Please," Lord Gregson whimpered. "I beg of you, stop."

"Do not doubt that if more word of you attacking innocent ladies emerges, I will find you again," he warned, before lashing him again. "I'll cut you up and feed you to a pack of wild dogs. Do you understand me?"

"Please." Lord Gregson was weeping like a babe.

"Tell me you understand." The whip cracked another time.

"I understand! I'll never do it again. I swear it!"

The desperation in the other man's voice was enough to persuade Rafe he may have finally managed to make some progress.

He brought the whip down a final time for good measure before tossing it to the floor. "Heed my warning, Lord Gregson, or I promise you, the next time won't go as easy."

With that warning, he stalked from the room, leaving the lord sobbing, welted, and bloody.

After another long, yet fulfilling, day of working with her charges, Persephone made her way to her room for the evening. Anne and Elizabeth continued to make marked strides in their reading and other lessons. She was quite pleased with the improvement they had shown, and during her daily visit to confer with Persephone over the girls' progress that evening, Lady Octavia had expressed her happiness as well. Mr. Sutton, who ordinarily accompanied his wife, had been absent.

She could not have been more fortunate to have discovered this post quite unexpectedly whilst living off the meager, dwindling wages she had been able to collect from her previous situation. It had certainly been the answer to her desperate prayers, and in more ways than one. Mr. Sutton and Lady Octavia were kind and thoughtful. They did not speak to her condescendingly as the Earl and Countess of Landsdowne had. They paid her fair wages and treated her as if she were a valued member of the household. They were never sparing in their praise, and nor did they cast judgment on her choice of lessons.

Admittedly, she had never expected to become a governess. When circumstances had forced her into the position to protect herself, she had been uncertain of what she was meant to be teaching. Her own governesses had been strict and stern, forcing her to walk with books balanced on her head, making her wear a corset to improve her posture, rapping her wrists with a rod when she did not please. But Persephone had no wish to implement the same tortures which had been inflicted upon her. She chose instead to instill a love of literature and learning which had been denied her. She was abysmal at needlework and water colors, it was true. Her governesses had all despaired over her fledgling abilities. Cousin Bartholomew had been appalled when he had checked upon her progress.

The work of a tyro, he had said dismissively, before firing her governess of the moment.

Although Persephone had not seen it then, she could discern quite plainly now that he had been attempting to groom her into being the wife he wished for himself. In his mind, it was simple. He would mold her, marry her, and absorb all her wealth for himself. But he had made one mistake in failing to realize she was not the sort of lady who would allow herself to be molded.

Thank heavens she had escaped him. All she needed to do was remain out of his reach until her birthday. And possibly beyond. But she would confront that matter later, when the necessity arose. For now, she was tired and comfortable and safe.

Or rather, as comfortable and safe as she could possibly feel given her tenuous position. Despite the kindness Rafe Sutton had shown her that day in the carriage, Persephone remained convinced it was only a matter of time before her lies were revealed. Whether unintentionally or out of an abundance of caution given that she was providing care for his nieces, she could not say. All she *did* know was that each morning, she woke with dread in her belly even as the sun rose high on the promise of a new day.

Undoubtedly, tomorrow would prove no different.

Persephone unleashed a wistful sigh as she reached the door to her room. Holding her taper aloft to illuminate the passage, she reached for the latch and pushed the door open, crossing over the threshold. The moment the portal closed at her back, however, she knew something was amiss.

The scent of the room was different.

Different, yet familiar.

Shaving soap and man and...

Rafe Sutton.

Freezing where she stood, she cast a wild glance about the shadows of her small room.

"Good evening, Miss Wren."

She wheeled about to find *him* behind her, his large form occupying the inkiness of the far corner of the room where a small chair dwelled. Often, the piece of furniture in question provided an excellent place to read in the morning before she needed to join Anne and Elizabeth for their first lessons of the day. It was her place, the only space in the entire town house which was solely hers. The only place that had *ever* seemed hers, in fact.

And now, Rafe Sutton was occupying it as if he belonged there.

"Mr. Sutton," she snapped, holding her free hand to her madly galloping heart. "What are you doing here?"

He made no move to stand. Instead, he waved his hand in a languid gesture which encompassed his body. "What am I doing here beneath this roof, or here in your room again?"

"Beneath this roof," she said hastily. "Or rather, in my room. Oh, bother. Both."

Her foolish gaze seized the opportunity to drink him in. His long legs were encased in trousers, his ankles crossed. His hazel eyes met hers through the murk, sending a spark of awareness straight through her, as burning as if it had been cast directly from a live flame. He wore no jacket this evening, she realized as she moved nearer, chasing the darkness with the soft, warm illumination of her candle. Instead, he was in his shirt sleeves and waistcoat, the knot of his snowy cravat loose at his throat.

Why did he have to be so wickedly alluring? There was something about the man that transcended mere looks. He simply exuded something that drew her to him in a way no man before him had. Or, she suspected, could.

"I am staying here."

The smooth, self-assured response had her instantly on edge.

"Here in my room?" she blurted, before inwardly chastising herself.

It could not be! Mr. Sutton and Lady Octavia would never allow such a scandalous arrangement. Her mind whirled. She was flustered. Her face hot. The rest of her body...*hotter*.

What was this flush that overcame her whenever he was near? Why and how? Could she put an end to it?

Rafe chuckled and unfolded his body from the chair,

rising to his full height. Curse him, but the sound was velvet and silk to her senses. Soft and smooth and decadent.

Rafe? When had she begun to think of him in such intimate terms?

"Beneath this roof, Miss Wren. My brothers and sisters and I are opening a new venture in the West End, The Sinner's Palace II. I'll be running the daily operations, which means I need to be closer than the East End more often than not."

Beneath.

This.

Roof?

He was staying *here*? Every night? Worry assailed her, mingling with the unwanted desire. Not fear about his presence, but rather for what it would mean to her in terms of the looming secret she had revealed.

"Have you told Mr. Sutton and Lady Octavia about what happened at my last situation?" she asked, trying to tamp down her body's frantic response.

He moved soundlessly, with the same innate grace she had noted before. Catlike and elegant and yet delightfully masculine all at once.

"Even if I were to tell Jasper and his wife that bastard Gregson attempted to force himself on you, they would find fault with that cowardly scoundrel, where it belongs," he said, his countenance serious, his gaze searching. "Surely you know that?"

"I forged my letter of character to gain this position," she said. "When I left Lord Landsdowne's home, I knew I would have to forfeit that, but I was also desperate."

"You did what you needed to do." Rafe removed the remainder of the distance between them, plucking the taper from her fingers before moving away to light a brace of candles and a small lamp.

More light flooded her room, and she was at once grateful for it and dismayed.

Grateful because her eyes no longer had to strain through the darkness to make out the beautiful symmetry of his face. Dismayed because her eyes no longer had to strain through the darkness to make out the beautiful symmetry of his face. And all the rest of him, too.

He was more handsome than she had recalled, if at all possible. Surely it was impossible, was it not? Certainly implausible. Yet, he was. She found herself moving toward him, seeking his warmth. Seeking his presence.

"I did what I had to do, yes, but I lied," she pointed out. "I lied to you. I lied to them. All you need to do is tell them my letter of character was forged, and they will ask me to leave without reference."

She was giving voice to her fears. Quite foolishly. And yet, the words had left her in a mad rush. When had Rafe Sutton become her confidante?

"I won't tell them, Miss Wren." Gently and slowly, as if he feared she were a wild creature who might start and flee, he reached out, running his forefinger beneath her jaw. The caress was so tender and fleeting, she would have believed she had imagined it if not for the tingling warmth where his bare skin had touched hers. "Will you tell me your name?"

"Persephone," she said, the only part of her that was not a lie. The only part of her that was truly hers to give him.

When she had escaped Cousin Bartholomew, she had known she would need to change her surname to render it more difficult to find her. It was a matter of course that he would come looking. He would not wish for his fortune to flee him. But she had kept her given name, not wanting to lose herself entirely.

She was still Persephone. She was merely no longer Lady Persephone Calcot.

"Persephone," Rafe repeated, a small grin quirking his lips, his dimples appearing. "Ah, how interesting."

"Interesting?" She was trying not to allow herself to be charmed by him and failing miserably.

She ought to tell him to leave her room instead of admiring the glint of the low light in his blond curls, and yet she could not. There was the faintest golden stubble of whiskers on his jaw that she found utterly mesmerizing.

"Hades and Persephone. I know the tale," he said, his smile fading and taking with it those maddening grooves that served to enhance his appeal. "Hades stole Persephone away to the underworld."

He ran his hand along the well-defined angle she had been admiring, and for a brief, mad moment, she wondered what it would feel like, what would happen if she were to replace his hand with hers.

Then, she banished the dangerous thought from her mind.

You're being foolish, Persephone. This man is not for you.

"I am afraid I fail to see what is interesting about the story," she forced herself to say. "It seems rather unbelievable, if you ask me. He fell in love with her after seeing her picking flowers? How trite."

Rafe raised a brow. "I reckon that for the right woman, a man might lose his heart and his head easily. He may even forgive a lady for slipping laudanum into his brandy."

A strange warmth invaded her. What was he suggesting? Surely not that he had lost either his head or his heart to her. That was impossible. He scarcely even knew her. And furthermore, she was still lying to him, even now. Her every waking moment was one falsehood after the next, perpetuated over and over, without end.

The guilt returned, heavy as a stone. "Perhaps you should not have forgiven me, Mr. Sutton."

"I'm a forgiving chap when forgiveness is due." His jaw clenched. "Not when it ain't. You can be sure Lord Gregson won't be trying to force himself on any other ladies any time soon. I've made certain of that."

Lord Gregson.

The mentioning of him had her entire body stiffening as if she had been struck. Slowly, Rafe's words permeated the intensity of her reaction.

"You've made certain?" She searched his countenance. "How?"

"I whipped his lily-white arse until he was bleeding and sobbing like a babe."

She blinked, certain he was jesting. But Rafe Sutton's expression remained solemn and imperturbable. "You... whipped him?"

Surely he knew he could be arrested for daring to strike the son of an earl.

"He deserved it." Half his mouth pulled up in a small grin that was sadly bereft of dimples.

"Something serious could befall you for doing so, Mr. Sutton."

"Eh." He waved a hand in dismissive fashion, as if he were chasing an irritating fly. "No need to worry on my account. I made certain the buffle-headed scoundrel hasn't a bloody inkling who gave him the drubbing. All 'e knows is why."

A rush of emotion swept over her, so overwhelming that her eyes began to sting with the precursor to tears. The knowledge he had done violence to Lord Gregson left her reeling with shock and a stirring sense of justice having been done.

But what to say in such a moment? It had been plain to Persephone, from the moment she had first met him, that Rafe Sutton was not the sort of gentleman who ordinarily graced Mayfair drawing rooms. His admission, however, was confirmation. He had whipped Lord Gregson.

Rafe's words echoed in her mind.

He deserved it.

Yes. He had deserved it. But no one had ever taken such a stand for her before. She'd never had a champion. All her life, she had been at the mercy of others. She blinked as her vision blurred with tears. They trickled down her cheeks, unstoppable.

"Ah Christ, lovely." Rafe extracted a handkerchief from his waistcoat and dabbed at her cheeks. "No need to cry over the fate of such a piece of shite."

His gesture, so tender and unexpected, and in complete disparity to the viciousness of the act he had perpetuated upon the viscount, made her tears flow anew.

She sniffed but held herself still, accepting his ministrations. "I am not weeping over Lord Gregson."

A frown creased his brow. "Why, then?"

"Because no one has ever championed me." The admission was humiliating.

A woman grown, four-and-twenty years of age, and not one soul had ever cared about what had become of her. Aside from when she had run away from Cousin Bartholomew, she did not expect he had ever given her much consideration. And before that…well, she had no memories of her mother or father.

"Bleeding hell," Rafe swore. "Then you've never known anyone who *deserved* to know you."

The most ridiculous urge to throw her arms about him rose within her. To hold him tight, breathe in his scent and bask in his nearness. But how strange, when she had never embraced another in her life, aside from her charges. And oh, what a blessing the exuberant hugs of Anne and Elizabeth were. Although not the same.

Not a man's embrace.

Not Rafe Sutton's arms circling her waist.

Would he embrace her in return?

"Thank you," she said, and then she gave in to the desire.

One step was all it took. One step, and she was pressed against him from breast to hip. Her movement was so sudden and awkward, she nearly upset their balances and sent the both of them crashing to the floor. She wrapped her arms around his neck and buried her face in the soft linen of his simply tied cravat. He held her against him, and unless she was mistaken, he pressed his nose to her crown. She inhaled deeply, wanting to commit the scent of him to memory. To remember always the warmth and vitality he exuded. To preserve this moment so that she could return to it in her mind and be newly astounded by the rush of feeling.

"You needn't thank me, lovely," he rasped.

Lovely, he had called her for the second time. She could not lie—she liked the way it sounded in his deep, smoky baritone, with his accent that was not quite proper, just a bit raw and rough and...*real*. Just *him*.

And then the sweetest gesture of all—his lips pressed to her part. He had kissed her. Rafe Sutton, East End charmer, had sought vengeance against Lord Gregson for her, and then he had dried her tears, held her in his arms, and kissed her. Not on her lips, where others had forced kisses she had not wanted in the past. But in that previously unconsidered place, the top of her head.

He was a complex and mysterious man, and she knew in that moment that if there was anything she must do when in his presence, it was to guard her heart. Rafe Sutton was the sort of goodhearted rogue a woman could fall in love with. And she very much could not afford such a folly.

One moment more, Persephone.

Or two.

One, two, three...

Let go of him, you fool.

With another sniffle, she released her hold on him and stepped away, feeling both bereft and embarrassed by her display of emotion.

"Thank you," she repeated, for it was necessary, and words, in this instance, were insufficient. "I suppose we should both get our rest, then."

"We should," he agreed, tucking his handkerchief back into the pocket of his waistcoat with a nod.

She thought of his cravat which she had discovered the morning after he had slept in her bed. Likely, she ought to return it to him, and yet, she found herself strangely reluctant to relinquish the scrap of starched linen, pitifully wrinkled by its presence beneath her pillow.

And the number of times you have extracted it and held it to your nose for a hint of his scent.

"I bid you good evening, Mr. Sutton," she said, hating the words, hating putting an end to their time together, and yet knowing she must.

For her own self-preservation, if nothing else.

"Call me Rafe," he said, that rogue's smile of his firmly back in place. "Good evening, Persephone."

With a bow, he was gone.

And she stood in her room alone, arms hugging her waist, wondering why she had never felt her loneliness in such acute fashion until now.

CHAPTER 6

*R*afe woke in the wee hours of the morning in a strange bed, unable to sleep.

Thinking of *her*.

The governess.

Persephone.

She was one staircase and thirty-seven steps away from him. Not that he had been counting…

Oh, Christ. Who was he fooling?

He had counted. Of bloody course he had. Both on his way there the previous evening and on his return to the guest chamber Lady Octavia had assigned him.

On a snort, Rafe threw back the bedclothes, rising from the bed. And fancy that, a guest chamber. It sounded like something some spoiled lordling would inhabit. Suttons were not meant to live in Mayfair and observe proprieties and mingle with ladies and lords, earls and viscounts, and dukes and marchionesses.

Suttons had been born to the stink and the sadness of the rookeries, and that was where they were meant to remain. At least, that was what Rafe had always believed. Until Jasper had married Lady Octavia and settled his family here. In fucking Mayfair!

He poured cold water into a basin and splashed his face, performing his morning ablutions. The reaction Persephone had given to the news he had exacted vengeance upon Viscount Gregson for what he had done to her had been surprising. He had not anticipated tears, gratitude, or such a physical response. And curse him if he could not still imagine her body pressed to his, her arms around his neck, the sweet scent of her invading his senses. Summer, sunshine, flowers, glorious, beautiful life...*Persephone*.

Damn it, perhaps living at his brother's town house to help ease the burden of moving between The Sinner's Palace and the second Sinner's Palace had been a terrible idea. In fact, he knew it had been. Because temptation was here.

And temptation's name was Miss Persephone Wren.

Temptation had sunset hair, eyes that were warm and brown with hints of cinnamon and gold, and breasts he could not help but to imagine burying his face—or cock—between, and she was tall. They were nearly the same height.

A long Meg.

A delectable one.

His for the taking.

No, what the devil was he thinking? He could not seduce Persephone. Rafe reached for a towel and blotted his face, neck and hands. She had already been mistreated by far too many arseholes, and she deserved better. A woman like Miss Wren was the sort a man married, not the sort he shagged.

And Rafe wasn't the kind of chap who longed to find himself leg-shackled. His life was plummy the way it was. He was happy tending to his family's gaming hells and bedding whomever he bleeding liked.

Reminding himself of that often would likely be a necessity if he stayed here in Mayfair for too long, the temptation of Persephone too close for comfort.

On a sigh, he finished dressing and then left his chamber, a lone taper accompanying him to illuminate the way since the hour was so early, even the servants were still abed. May as well get a start to his day. He had an endless mountain of work awaiting him. The Sinner's Palace II was, quite unlike its predecessor, a West End affair. For the rich culls who didn't dare venture to the stews. For earls and dukes and marquesses and mayhap even princes. This was to be their true beginning. A solidification of their family's power and influence.

And he could not bloody wait for the doors to open, the tables filling with arrogant, soft-palmed lords ready to lose their papa's coin. Grinning at the thought, Rafe descended the stairs and stalked down the hall. He supposed he would leave through the mews. He did not think he would ever grow accustomed to Jasper having a butler and footmen and all manner of fart catchers, and he could do for himself as well as any coachman or groom.

He was almost at the end of the hall when he noted light flickering from beneath a door. Curiosity and suspicion mingling, he decided to investigate. This was Mayfair, yes, but that fact had not deterred trouble from finding its way here.

He extracted the blade he always kept secreted in his boot, thinking he may have inadvertently stumbled upon a thief, attempting to filch something of value. Slowly, he opened the door to the library, peering through the crack to determine his next course of action.

What he found within, however, was not a thief.

Rather, it was the woman he had not been able to stop thinking about. His troublesome cock was already rising to attention at the sight of her, curled in a chair by the fireplace, a brace of candles on the table at her side, a book in her lap. He tucked his knife inside the sheath in his boot.

Christ, she was asleep, her head tilted back.

She was going to get a cramp in her neck.

Rafe told himself that was the reason he was crossing the threshold and carpets to where she sat instead of leaving through the mews as he had intended. He most definitely was not rushing to her side because the scent of her had been taunting him all night long and he was desperate for one more sniff. Or because he was desperate for any excuse to be in her presence.

He placed his taper on the table beside her, then plucked the open tome from her lap. Curious, he glanced down to find it was written in a language he didn't recognize. Latin? French? He could not be certain. All he did know was that his Persephone was a damned intelligent wench.

His Persephone?

He needed to pull his head out of his arse. What was the matter with him? No woman had ever affected him thus before, and he didn't like it. Not at all.

He snapped the book closed and placed it on the table as well, taking a moment to drink in the sight of her, face relaxed in slumber. All the starch was gone from her shoulders, and she hardly looked prim with her legs curled beneath her bottom, her curves accentuated by a dressing gown that did nothing to hide the ample blessings of her breasts and hips.

What he wouldn't give to worship every inch of her body with his tongue.

You're dicked in the nob, Rafe Sutton.

"Persephone," he said softly, not wanting to give her a start but also knowing he needed to wake her before he spent the next hour watching her sleep like a lovesick pup who had never seen a quim before.

She shifted and made a sleepy sound of contentment that made his prick twitch.

"Persephone," he tried again, this time touching her shoulder.

Her eyes fluttered open. "Rafe?"

Her frown of puzzlement was adorable, damn it. He would give his left arm to kiss her.

Stop touching her, you horse's arse.

But she was so warm, searing his palm and fingers and he could not seem to stop now that he had begun. "You were sleeping."

"Oh dear. What a waste of Mr. Sutton's candles." She jolted upright in her seat, the tension which had become a familiar sight returning to her shoulders. "I should never have come here."

Reluctantly, he withdrew his hand from her shoulder, offering it instead for her to pull herself up. "The hour is quite early. You ought to return to your bed for some sleep."

"Thank you for waking me. I never intended to fall asleep here."

Her hand settled in his, and from the moment their bare flesh connected, he recognized the mistake he had made. But it was too late now. She may as well have touched him with flame. Her dainty fingers wrapped around his callused digits. He never wanted to let her go.

By all the saints, he wanted to pull her into his arms and keep her there.

He drew her to her feet instead, the scent of her Winter's soap tantalizing him. The hem of her dressing gown brushed his trousers.

"What bloody language is that book?" he asked to distract himself from her intoxicating proximity.

"Latin," she said, a soft smile curving her lips. "I taught it to myself, for my governesses never taught me because... Oh, it scarcely matters now."

"Governesses?" He searched her countenance, wondering, not for the first time, about her background.

Surely most women in her circumstance had landed there out of necessity, and likely were not the sorts of ladies who would have once had governesses of their own. And he did not think he was mistaken in that she had been about to say something she had thought better of.

Miss Persephone Wren had secrets. He was willing to wager everything he owned on it. And he wanted to know them all.

"Yes," she said simply, instead of offering the detailed explanation he would have preferred. "Governesses."

"I thought governesses were for fancy ladies. Daughters of earls and rich coves and such." Their hands were still linked. He was reluctant to release her, though he knew she must be tired.

"Ordinarily." Her pink tongue stole from beneath the seam of her lips, sweeping over her Cupid's bow.

She had done nothing to sate his curiosity. It would seem she wanted to keep her secrets. And his lust would not be sated either. It was time to go. He had done his duty and awakened her that she might garner a bit more sleep before her day began.

Rafe forced himself to drop her hand, but the loss of her touch was a physical ache.

He tamped down the longing and offered her a bow. "Good morrow, Miss Wren."

Frustrated with himself, he reached for his taper.

"What were you doing in the library at this hour of the morning?" she asked him primly.

Providing him a reason to linger for another moment.

He gave her his best smile, the one that never failed to

charm the ladies. "I spied a glow beneath the door when I was on my way to the mews."

Her gaze searched his. "Where are you going?"

"Across the sea," he quipped lightly. "Would you like to accompany me?"

"Yes," she surprised him by saying. "I very much would. I think it unlikely any of my woes would follow me that far."

"And what woes does a beautiful governess have?" He thought of what Gregson had done to her and could have kicked himself. "Aside from the one I whipped bloody on your behalf, that is."

Her countenance turned sad. "More than I wish to have. That is certain."

He did not begin to understand the protective surge he had for her. He wanted to carry her away and make sure she never knew a moment of harm again. And yet, how foolish that was. He scarcely even knew her.

Still, why did he feel as if he did, as if he always had, in the deepest sense?

"Any others in need of a whipping?" he asked, striving to keep his voice light, though he sensed a heaviness within her. A sadness. "I am more than happy to oblige."

"You never did say how you managed to be in a position to administer Lord Gregson's…reckoning," she said carefully.

What a polite phrasing she had. Still the dignified governess, though it was the early hours of the morning, her feet were bare, she was clad in nothing more substantial than a layer or two of fabric, and they were alone. Her hair was unbound, by God.

He had been too entranced by the rest of her to notice until now. How? He could not fathom it as he watched the candlelight glistening in her long locks.

He needed to end this dangerous turn of thought.

"My thrashing of him, you mean."

She nibbled at her lip, and he had to stifle a groan. "Yes. How did you do it?"

Well, hell. How to explain?

He raked his fingers through his hair, struggling for a proper answer. "It happened at an...er...a School of Venus."

One of the most sought-after, he might have added, for it would have been true. Where the depravities were a little more depraved than the rest of London. But such a revelation would scarcely earn the lady's admiration, would it?

Hell. Did he want her admiration?

Yes.

"A School of Venus?" Her brow furrowed.

"A nunnery," he clarified.

"You went to a nunnery for me?"

"It ain't that generous, lovely." He shifted his weight from one boot to the other, feeling deuced uncomfortable. "I'm familiar with the abbess."

Why in the devil's arsehole did you say that?

"But what was Lord Gregson doing with an abbess at a nunnery?"

Now he had done it. Miss Wren—Persephone—was such an innocent, she had no notion of what a nunnery was. Or why a man such as the despicable Gregson—or himself, for that matter—would seek out such a place.

"A bawdy house," he explained, feeling like an utter cad. The lowest of the low. *Lower* than the lowest of the low. "A nunnery is a bawdy house. The abbess is the bawd who oversees the whores."

There. He had told her all. Well, not the bit about Lord Gregson liking to be whipped by whores. No need to tell her everything he knew.

Her lips parted. Her expression was unreadable, a mix of shock and something else.

Curiosity?

Surely not.

This was the prim Miss Wren before him.

"You are familiar with the abbess," she said, repeating what he had just told her, only with a new tone of comprehension in her voice. "Does that mean you…*oh*. Is she your paramour?"

Ah, hell. "No. She is a friend."

He had never bedded Sophie. But this was hardly the sort of conversation he wished to have with Persephone.

"I see." She nodded, and that tongue of hers once more slid over her lower lip.

He swallowed. "Yes. Enough patter. I've a full day's work ahead of me."

The need to flee this conversation was strong. Being alone with her was a temptation he could not afford to indulge in for another moment. She had been through far too much with Gregson. She deserved to be wooed and courted and treated with the utmost of care, as if she were fashioned of finest silk. She was too good for a man of his sort, that was for damn sure. And explaining any more of his past to her would be bloody unpleasant.

He turned to go for the second time.

But her hand caught his coat sleeve, staying him yet again.

"Mr. Sutton," she said. "Rafe."

He turned back to her. "Yes, Miss Wren?"

He had to think of her as Miss Wren, the governess. Not Persephone, the sunset-haired siren. Then perhaps he could keep himself under control. Tamp down the relentless urge to kiss her senseless. To learn what those lips would feel like.

She closed the distance between them in a flurry of movement, her hands settling on his shoulders. And then, her mouth collided with his.

He had his answer.

Hot and soft as silk and heavenly.

His mouth was warm and plumper than she had expected, those supple lips matching to hers in a way that felt somehow as if it had been preordained. She had taken him by surprise with her ardor. But then, she had taken herself by surprise, too.

But his hesitation did not last long.

In an instant, his mouth was moving over hers, slowly, tenderly, as if he were savoring her. Persephone became aware of everything in a new way. His breath, hot and mingling with hers, the glide of his tongue in her mouth. His scent, fresh soap and musky man invading her senses. The settle of his hands on her waist. The brush of his too-long hair against her cheek. And his kisses.

God, his kisses. They were kisses of seduction rather than an exercise in power, masterful and smooth. He kissed her in a way she had never been kissed before, urging her to respond in turn with his lips and tongue.

Her entire body suffused with heat.

She had not intended to kiss him. It was rash and foolish and reckless to do so. But now that her mouth had met his, she could not stop. She was voracious with the need to consume and be consumed. His hands moved from her waist, sliding to the small of her back, pulling her nearer.

Into his tall, lean hardness.

For the first time since she had awoken to his form towering over her, she was reminded of how few layers of fabric separated her from him. No petticoats, no stays. She wore nothing but her night rail and a simple dressing gown, primly buttoned but not a sufficient barrier. However, unlike the other occasions in which she had found herself alone with a man, she did not feel even a hint of fear. Instead of the layers of fabric proving a protection, in Rafe Sutton's arms, they felt like an unwanted hindrance.

She had not known kissing could be so transformative.

It was as if, before her lips had touched his, she had been a different person. Someone timid and afraid. And now, in his arms, she had come to life. There had never been a reason to fear this man. He had defended her when no one else ever had.

He was a rake and a charmer, but one with a good heart.

She had been faced with a choice: allow him to walk away, or seize the moment. Kiss the handsome East End rogue, knowing she may never have another chance. Her body had made the decision for her, moving into his, against his, seeking more.

He made a low sound, part growl, part groan. How liberating to think this clever seducer affected by her untutored kiss. A sudden desperation seized her. He had been about to leave, but the world was still dark beyond the windows, bathed in shadows and secrets. The house was quiet and enrobed in the tranquility of the night, and no one would need to know…

Rafe gentled the kiss, brushing his lips over hers once, twice, then rubbing his lower lip over the upper bow of hers. For a brief, worried moment, she thought he would stop, take his mouth from hers. But then he found the corner of her lips, dragging his kiss over her cheek. One of his hands abandoned her back, his fingers instead sinking into her unbound hair, cupping the base of her skull and urging her head to fall back. Tenderly pulling her in the direction he wished.

She trusted him, she realized. Implicitly. In a way she had not trusted another. Was it his ruthless securing of vengeance on her behalf? Or was it something else? Persephone could not say.

All she could do was allow him to move her as he wanted, exposing her throat to him.

He nuzzled her ear, then pressed a kiss to the whorl. Her breaths were ragged, coming faster. Her lips tingled with the memory of his. She rubbed her cheek against his and closed her eyes, savoring this stolen embrace, perhaps the only she would ever have.

Rafe kissed down her neck, his mouth setting her skin alight. It was too much and not enough all at once. His arm wrapped more firmly around her waist when her knees trembled, anchoring her to him and keeping her from sliding to a heap upon the carpets. That was when she felt the evidence of his body's reaction, the thick hardness prodding her.

She opened her eyes, taking in the sight of him, wrapped in her embrace.

She knew what it was, that prominent ridge, but the revelation did not send an icy rush of foreboding through her as it had before, that terrible night when Lord Gregson had almost taken her against her will. Instead, it sent an answering pulse of need between her thighs.

This was different.

Rafe was different.

In his arms, she was safe.

Relief mingled with desire. She was not broken. Lord Gregson could not hurt her. Her hands took on a life of their own, learning Rafe's body. The broad shoulders, the muscled arms, the strength of his back. He opened his mouth and suckled her flesh in a place she had never known was so sensitive—the hollow at the base of her throat.

An embarrassing sound emerged, part squeak, part mewl.

Her fingers clutched at his coat, kneading the muscle and sinew beneath, begging him to never stop what he was doing. She wanted to wrap herself around him and hold him here, with his mesmerizing mouth and his deliciously wicked seduction.

Her life thus far had been a misery. Why not find the happiness where she could, when she could?

She was lost, awash in sensation and longing, her need for this man primitive.

"Persephone." He said her name as if it were the highest praise. As if she were a deity and he was worshipping at her altar.

His mouth moved, bestowing kisses wherever it went. Over her breasts. He kissed her there, too, where the peaks were stiff and hungry, rising beneath the layers of fabric separating her bare skin from his lips. She ought to have been ashamed of her response, the obviousness of her desire, but she forgot to care entirely when his lips opened over the tip of her breast, and he sucked her nipple.

"Oh." The lone word left her, all she could manage. Scarcely coherent.

With each draw, an answering desire tugged between her legs. She pressed herself against him, needing to be closer. No amount of proximity seemed as if it could ever be enough. His eyes were closed, the fan of his golden lashes falling over his cheeks in perfect symmetry. The hand that had been on the small of her back slid to her waist, then glided upward. He cupped her other breast, his thumb swirling over the nipple as he continued to tease her with suction and then light, little licks.

Softer than gossamer, the play of his tongue over her. His tender care, like his championing of her, turned Persephone's insides molten. No one had ever touched her with such reverence, and she knew instinctively that no one else ever would.

Nor would she desire them to.

What was it about this man, Rafe Sutton?

It hardly matters, does it? He is not for you. This stolen, forbidden moment in the pre-dawn library is all you shall ever have.

She was taunting herself. Her mind knew this was wrong, but her heart wanted it to go on forever. Her heart longed for when she was five-and-twenty and Cousin Bartholomew did not loom over her, a menace from which she could not escape.

Rafe released her nipple, kissing the side of her breast before raising his head, his eyes opening to meet hers. "Bleeding hell, I can't be doing this with you. You're an innocent, a governess. I'm no better than Gregson."

She was about to argue when the sound of voices and the telltale creak of footsteps in the hall reached her. A frantic glance toward the windows overlooking the street showed the undeniable glow of morning light filtering in. Heavens! She had been kissing him for so long she had lost all sense of time.

And now, the servants were moving about.

Which meant...

"Fucking hell," Rafe swore, keeping his voice low as he set her apart from himself. "I can't be caught here with you like this. It'll ruin you."

His concern for her would have warmed her at any other time, but now that his mouth had ceased weaving its spell over her, rational thought was beginning to return. She needed this position. She needed to remain hidden here, out of Cousin Bartholomew's reach, for another two months. Everything depended upon it.

"I will go first," she said, desperation taking command. "Wait until you can be certain no one will see you, and then you can leave."

How calm she sounded, when inside, she was anything but. Kissing the sinfully handsome brother of her employer was not a habit of hers. Nor was such recklessness. She would have given herself to him. And she would not have regretted it, either.

But she had no wish to lose her post. Forging another letter of character and finding a new situation was more trouble she did not need to invite.

"Forgive me, Miss Wren. I never should 'ave touched you," he rasped, looking as torn as he sounded.

The loss of his *h* was telling.

His reaction would have crushed her had she not been so desperate to flee. She took up the brace of candles and bolted without offering him a proper farewell, desperate to leave the library and return to the haven of her rooms, where no one could find fault with her actions.

It was only when she was safely within that she allowed herself to wonder which was worse, her willingness to be ruined, or his regret over what they had done.

CHAPTER 7

*R*egret filled Rafe's mouth with a bitter taste as he stalked along the pavements. There was no excuse for what he had done. None worth a damned scrope. No denying it or trying to make it sound any better than what it was.

He had lingered in the library long enough to make certain no servants saw him leaving the same room she had exited. Ruining a governess was out of the question. He'd avoided the parson's mousetrap thus far, and he'd continue evading it. And after what she had endured at the hands of Lord Gregson at her previous post, how could he defend all but seducing her this morning?

He could not. Nor could he excuse the start to the day. In lingering with Miss Wren, he had failed to realize the sun had risen, and it was past time for his arrival at the club. The work awaiting him would not finish itself.

The plain and awful truth of it was that he had almost fucked his nieces' governess in his brother's fancy Mayfair library. Had the interruption of the servants not occurred, he would likely still be there, tangled up in her, ballocks deep.

And what a place to be. Paradise, for certain.

He banished the unworthy thought.

This morning had not been one of his proudest moments, Rafe had to admit. Seducing a servant, and one who had previously been the victim of a vile lordling, was not his ordinary modus operandi. Hell, he had never done anything like that in his life. Innocents were not to his taste. Nor were ladies who spoke with crisp accents and could read fluent Latin and wore prim dressing gowns buttoned almost to their chins.

To do penance, he had forced himself to walk the distance from Jasper's Mayfair town house to the site of the new gaming hell he and his family would soon be opening. He was no stranger to sinning and the furthest one could reasonably find from a saint, but even he knew he had done wrong.

So why could he not cease thinking about her response to his kiss? Why was his mind still haunted by the way her lips had moved against his, so sweetly hesitant at first, and then with greater confidence and enthusiasm? *Devil take it.* Although the hour was early and the morning was chilly and damp, this vein of thought was heating his blood and proving dangerous, if not disastrous.

She had kissed him first, it was true. But he was no green virgin. He should have resisted the urge to kiss her, to slide his tongue inside the satiny warmth of her mouth. To not have lingered, putting his lips on every part of her he dared, including the pebbled bud of her nipple. He still cursed the layers that had kept him from the warmth of her flesh.

Even so, her moan of appreciation would echo in his mind to his dying day as the single most erotic sound he had ever heard. He was certain of it.

Scowling, he stepped inside The Sinner's Palace II, forcing his mind to where it belonged: work. This establishment was going to be grander, bolder, bigger, and infinitely more lucrative than its original. All he needed to do was recall why he was in the West End. And it wasn't to seduce Persephone Wren, damn it. She wasn't for him, and thinking about her wasn't going to line his bleeding purse.

He tried to summon a smile as he was greeted by the men who had been engaged to rehang the wall coverings. What a scoundrel he was. He'd had no right to return her kiss, no right to feast on her creamy throat or suck her nipple.

Irritation rose as he nodded to the men and stalked deeper into the labyrinth which was still in the process of being turned into the well-oiled machine The Sinner's Palace was. Fortunately, his siblings were aiding him in this endeavor.

From around the corner, raised voices reached him, one of them familiar. Speaking of siblings...

Rafe stalked into what would be the main gaming room of their establishment. To his surprise, his sister Pen, who was overseeing the decoration of The Sinner's Palace II, was in the center of the chamber having a heated discussion with one of the tradesmen. Auburn-haired like their brother Logan, Pen was quick to flush when she was angered or embarrassed. And given her stance and the loudness of her voice, Rafe was willing to wager she was the former rather than the latter.

She was not meant to be here today, curse it. He was going to have to discover just how she had arrived this morning. If she had dared to travel alone from the East End, he would give her an earful.

She paused when she spied him, relief coloring her voice. "Rafe, come here if you please, and explain to Mr. Waters why we cannot have inferior table cloths at our establishment. I have brought him here to show him the precise locations of the tables, and he now insists he cannot have the embroidery we require within the next month."

Embroidery?

Hell.

She was taking her role seriously, was she not?

"Mr. Sutton," the linen draper greeted, sounding relieved. "Perhaps you can provide the voice of reason, sir. Miss Sutton's demands are, regretfully, nigh impossible to achieve."

He very much doubted it. But the distraction would prove useful.

He looked from Pen to Mr. Waters. "What's the problem?"

"I want all the table cloths to be embroidered with a palace," Pen said, her voice taking on the same mulish cast as her expression.

No one was more stubborn than Pen when she was in fine dudgeon.

"A palace embroidered on each cloth?" he repeated, passing his hand along his jaw as he imagined how dear a price such a table linen would fetch.

"Only think how it will set us apart from our competitors," Pen declared.

He rather doubted the drunken lords and merchants who would haunt these halls would give a damn about whether or not the tablecloths were embroidered. Perhaps Pen was taking her role a mite *too* seriously.

"I have all the linens you originally purchased at the ready," Mr. Waters was saying. "But as for the embroidery, I must ask for an increase of price and far more time. I won't be capable of producing the number requested with the embroidery before you open your establishment, and Miss Sutton refuses to accept this."

"I won't accept it because your excuse simply isn't good enough, Mr. Waters," Pen said. "If you refuse to give us what we need, then we will take our business to someone who will."

Damn it, Pen was buzzing like an angry bee this morning. Waters was one of the finest linen drapers in London, and persuading him to sell his fine tablecloths to the Suttons for a gaming hell had required an extra greasing of the palm. It had hardly been the first time Rafe had used bribery to get what he wanted, and he had no doubt it would not be the last. But now Pen was doing her best to undo all the good work he had accomplished.

"You ought to consider yourself fortunate to have Waters and Sons linen gracing your tables," the draper said coldly, reinforcing Rafe's concerns.

"We will accept the linens you've already agreed to provide, Mr. Waters," he said smoothly, hoping to avoid further argument between Pen and the linen draper.

By God, he already had an aching head.

Which, he supposed, was only mildly better than an aching cock. At least this distraction, vexing as it was, had served to distract him from thoughts of Persephone and what could have happened in the library.

"We most certainly will not!" Pen snapped, outraged. "Mr. Waters, you can take your pompous airs and your plain tablecloths and stuff them up your—"

"That is enough, Penelope!" he barked, interrupting her tirade before she could finish. "Please excuse my sister, sir. Our order remains the same."

Flashing his most charming grin, he hastened to escort Mr. Waters from the room before Pen caused any more trouble with her antics. He exchanged a few more pleasantries and reassurances with the draper before returning to find his sister in tears.

Ah, hell. He could not abide by women turning on the waterworks. It made him devilishly uncomfortable.

"What is amiss, Pen?" he demanded, crossing the room in hasty strides.

He did not think he had ever seen Pen weep before. First her ridiculous requests, then her outrage with Mr. Waters, and now she was sobbing? Just what the floating hell was wrong with her this bleeding morning?

"How dare you undermine me?" she demanded through her tears. "He had the number of tablecloths wrong, and I fail to understand why he cannot provide the embroidery. He asked me where *Mr. Sutton* was when he arrived."

A fresh wave of tears punctuated her words.

He reached into his coat and extracted a handkerchief, offering it to her. "You need to calm yourself, Pen. The tables will be filled regardless of whether or not there is a bit of thread stitched in a palace on them."

She snatched the mouchoir from him and dabbed frantically at her cheeks. "Men are nothing but a great bloody lot of arrogant loggerheads!"

Ah.

"Is this about Lord Aidan Weir, Pen?" he asked.

"Of course not." She sniffled. "It's his brother the haughty arse who…"

Rafe's suspicions rose. "His brother? Which one?"

If he had to issue a warning to another member of the Weir family, he would. And gladly, too. Just what the devil *had* Pen been doing?

Pen shook her head. "It hardly matters now. I'll not be seeing Lord Lindsey again."

Lindsey? The viscount was the most notorious stickler of fashionable society.

He frowned, wondering how Pen would have crossed paths with the man. "That is for the best, sister."

"Of course it is," she agreed, smiling with unnatural cheer.

"But never mind his high and mighty lordship. We have a gaming hell to open."

"Indeed we do, and we'd both do well to keep our minds on The Sinner's Palace II where they belong," he said, as much for his own sake as hers.

"This is a most unusual matter, and I hesitate to even bring it to your attention," Mr. Jasper Sutton said, pity lacing his voice and countenance both.

Persephone's heart ceased to beat.

At least, that was what it felt like, so swift and fierce was her alarm.

Her spine stiffened and she sat up straighter in her seat. At first, she had believed the unexpected interview with her employer was so he might inquire, as he periodically did, after the improvements of his daughters in their lessons. When she had initially met the girls, they had been learning to read for the first time, but in the weeks she had known them, they had surpassed her greatest hopes. They were naturally intelligent and blessed with a stubborn determination that stood them in great stead.

However, it was apparent he had not called her here to discuss Anne and Elizabeth.

Which only meant one thing.

Someone had seen her leaving the library early this morning, disheveled and flushed from Rafe's kisses. They must have also spied him leaving shortly after. She had hoped he would be able to avoid detection as she had believed she had, but now, it would appear she had been mistaken.

"Forgive me for my intrusion in the library, sir," she rushed to say, hoping she might persuade him that nothing untoward had occurred. "I had been unable to sleep last night on account of some dreams which have been plaguing me, and I wandered from my room in search of something to read. Unfortunately, I fell asleep while reading. I would never have allowed the candles to burn for so long unattended. If you wish to remove the cost from my wages, I shall understand. As for Mr. Sutton, I can assure you that he was doing nothing more than being a gentleman, after having found me sleeping in the chair. He awoke me so that I might seek the comfort of my room instead. No propriety was breached."

As the mad burst of words came to a halt, she became aware Mr. Jasper Sutton was looking at her with an odd expression on his face. The pity had been replaced by surprise.

He drummed his fingers idly on the surface of the desk behind which he sat, his inkwell and papers spread before him. "The library, Miss Wren?"

Her mouth went dry as a new, different wave of panic struck. "Is that not what you wished to speak with me about, Mr. Sutton?"

The movement of his fingers continued in a steady pattern. *Tap tap tap tap. Tap tap tap tap.* Aside from his fingertips on the desk, silence reigned. For an indeterminate span of time, Mr. Jasper Sutton did not answer, his searching hazel gaze—so like his brother's—pinning her in place where she sat.

"You were in the library with Mr. Sutton," he said slowly, rather than answering her question. "With Mr. Rafe Sutton, my brother?"

She swallowed a steadily rising knot of worry. "Yes, Mr. Rafe Sutton. Your brother, sir."

Lord in heaven, had no one seen them? And had she just foolishly admitted to being alone with Rafe in the library desperately early this morning?

"He behaved in a gentlemanly fashion toward you, Miss Wren?" Mr. Sutton asked, frowning.

His manner was not usually so serious and stern. When she saw him with Anne and Elizabeth or with Lady Octavia, he was quite soft-spoken, given to smiling, not at all rigid. But there was a foreboding quality about him now, emanating from him, that filled her with dread.

"The perfect gentleman," she responded, hating herself for the suddenly high-pitched nature of her voice. Almost a squeak, if she were honest with herself.

"I don't suppose my brother and the word *gentleman* have ever gone along together before this little patter of ours," Mr. Jasper Sutton said.

He did not believe her. And he was not wrong to cast doubt upon her tale. Rafe had been tender and gentle and sweet, but he had not been a gentleman in the expected sense of the word. A gentleman would never have kissed her in return, would never have held her close or pressed his lips to her throat.

But she was heartily glad he had not been a gentleman on this occasion, and that he had done all those things.

She shifted in her chair, desperately uncomfortable. "In this instance, it is quite suiting, I assure you."

Yet another lie, but what was one more in an endless swell of so many?

She thought of his lips moving along her cheek, traveling down her neck, closing over her nipple and sucking. When she had finally arrived back at her room, she had discovered a wet spot there, over her still aching nipple, from him. She had felt like a wanton, and yet she had also felt undeniably pleased.

"Hmm," was all Jasper Sutton said, his fingers still methodically dropping atop the desk. "I shall take you at your word, Miss Wren. The library ain't my reason for asking you here, however."

He spoke very much like Rafe, she noted for the first time. Polished and intentional accents with the occasional rawness. Perhaps a bit more of it even than Rafe possessed. But she was less concerned with the comparison between the two brothers than she was with the true reason Mr. Jasper Sutton had summoned her to his study for an interview.

"If I may be so bold, Mr. Sutton, what was the reason?" she asked, worry lacing through her anew.

"Viscount Gregson," he said.

A name, nothing more.

She froze, lips and heart and mind going numb.

"What of him?" she forced herself to ask.

"He claimed to have been…uniquely humiliated in your name," Mr. Sutton said. "He came to The Sinner's Palace in a rage."

"How did he know I am in your employ?" she asked, startled by the notion that the viscount had found her with such ease.

If he had done so, then surely Cousin Bartholomew might as well, supposing he learned she was calling herself Persephone Wren and working as a governess.

"I inquired with his father, Lord Landsdowne, concerning the letter of character he provided for you."

Oh good heavens. She had not supposed he had done so. Her deception had been bold and risky, but it had been her only choice. But it was apparent that if he had inquired with the earl, then he must have also discovered she had forged the letter.

"Yes," Mr. Sutton said, as if he had access to the thoughts frantically wheeling through her mind. "I'm aware the document wasn't written by the earl. He was displeased by the manner in which you left and made no secret of it."

Her fingers twisted in the fabric of her gown but she forced herself to remain otherwise still. "How long have you known?"

Mr. Sutton inclined his head. "Since the first week you joined us. I ain't the sort of chap who doesn't believe in second chances, Miss Wren. But I also protect what's mine. The penmanship on your letter was too damned flowery to belong to a cove, so I investigated."

He had known from almost the beginning of her tenure here. It seemed impossible that he would know she had lied and yet keep her on.

"Nothing to say, Miss Wren?" he asked gently. "No need to look cow-hearted. I won't be dismissing you over the letter of character."

"You won't?"

"Landsdowne is a bag of wind. Never cared for his opinion on anything. I only tolerate the man at my establishment because I like his coin. I've been watching you with Anne and Elizabeth, as has my wife. I trust our judgment far more."

Lord Landsdowne *was* a blustery sort of fellow. And his son was even more despicable. The differences between her former employer and Mr. Sutton and Lady Octavia could not be more disparate.

"Thank you, sir." Her relief was tentative, for there was more to this dialogue, another reason why she had been called before him.

Gregson's whipping.

She swallowed.

"Gregson demanded an audience with you," Mr. Sutton said.

Panic hit her with the force of a blow. For a moment, she could not catch her breath. The thought of once more facing him made bile rise in her throat. "Please, Mr. Sutton, do not require that of me."

"No fears on that account either, Miss Wren. I don't invite swine beneath my roof. This ain't a barn."

She would have smiled were she not so desperately on edge, fearful of what he would say next. "I am relieved, sir. However, I am uncertain what you want from me concerning this matter."

His fingers gave another slow, rhythmic drum, and he watched her once more, with that calculating gaze that told her he was as shrewd as he seemed and that he saw far more than those around him wished for him to see.

"After I learned what had happened to Gregson, I found myself curious, Miss Wren. I made some inquiries."

She glanced down at her lap, startled to discover her fingers were white with tension, and that she had nearly twisted her skirts into knots. "If you wish to dismiss me, Mr. Sutton, I understand."

Although Gregson had attempted to force himself on her, there was a stain cast upon her virtue solely because of her sex. In her former life, she would have been compromised. Ruined. Lord Gregson would have had to wed her to save his honor and protect her reputation. In her new life, as Persephone Wren, a governess prayed she could move to her next situation bereft of the shame that accompanied such terrible circumstances.

"I'll not be dismissing you, Miss Wren," Mr. Sutton said, his voice gentling. "All I want is an answer. Just what the devil is between you and my brother Rafe?"

It was a fair question.

If only she knew the answer.

Nothing? Everything?

Looking back up at her employer, she thought about what had happened earlier that day and she could not control the warmth flaring in her cheeks. "Nothing, sir. As I said, Mr. Sutton has been a gentleman on the rare occasions when he was in my presence."

Mr. Sutton raised a dark brow. "The morning after Lady Octavia was attacked, Anne and Elizabeth reported to us that Uncle Rafe told them Miss Wren was sleeping and that they weren't to tell. As I recall, he also urged them to remind me of something in a similar vein as what you just said, that he is a gentleman. I ought to have addressed it when the incident was fresh, but your conduct has been excellent, and I was hoping the matter would take care of itself. Given what I have recently heard, I must ask."

Yes, she supposed he must. Mr. Sutton was speaking of the morning Rafe had slept in her bed.

After she had slipped the laudanum into his brandy. What a terrible coil in which she found herself.

"I overslept that morning," she lied, desperate to remain here. "Forgive me, sir. I believe Mr. Sutton agreed to help find me for the twins, but I was yet abed. The excitement of the day before had quite overset me, though it is no excuse."

Just a bit more time. That was all she needed to be free.

"That is all, Miss Wren?" Mr. Sutton asked, his voice sharp, with a commanding edge.

"Yes, Mr. Sutton, sir," she said, struggling to hold his gaze. "That is all."

And that is a terrible prevarication.

"You may go, Miss Wren," he said. "But please do yourself a kindness and stay far away from Lord Gregson and my brother both."

She nodded. "Of course, Mr. Sutton. You have my word."

But she also had a feeling part of her word was about to be broken, for Rafe called to her in a way she was not sure she could resist.

Even should he prove her downfall.

CHAPTER 8

*R*afe returned to Jasper's town house at an hour that was deliberately late. The rest of the house was abed, only the servants about.

Just what he wanted.

Nay, what he *needed* for his own self-preservation. If he were to spy even the slightest glimpse of Persephone, he was not certain he could trust himself. To that end, he had dined and finished conducting all his business prior to his return. On the morrow, he would need to return to The Sinner's Palace II for another day of coordinating tradesmen and keeping Pen from turning on the waterworks. But after that, he had determined he would switch roles with his brother Hart, who had been running The Sinner's Palace floor. Hart could stay in the West End and rub elbows with ladies, which would please him mightily.

Meanwhile, Rafe could return to where he belonged and forget all about the mysterious and equally delectable governess who had somehow cast a spell over him he could not shake.

Pleased with himself for avoiding her and settling upon a

solution to his current problem of uncontrollable lust for a lady he could not shag, he crossed the threshold into his guest room.

And promptly discovered the source of what ailed him awaiting him, wearing a prim governess's gown that did nothing to detract from her loveliness.

What in the devil's arsehole was he to do with this development?

Rafe closed the door at his back and stalked across the fine carpets, irritated with himself for the way his heart hammered faster in his chest and his stupid prick twitched to life. "What are you doing in here?" he demanded.

His question emerged harsher than he had intended, for she flinched. "Forgive me for intruding, but I was hoping for a word with you, in private. This seemed the best way to ensure privacy."

Privacy. With her.

Lord in heaven, what he could do with this woman, a closed door, and a bed just waiting to be defiled.

Calm yourself, you bleeding reprobate.

"This ain't the place for it," he ground out, taking her elbow in a firm grip and intending to haul her from the room.

"Please, Rafe," she pleaded, putting up some opposition rather than allowing herself to be dragged nicely across the room as he had hoped she might. "I only need a moment of your time. Every minute I spend here risks my position, which I fear has already grown quite tenuous given what I heard from Mr. Sutton today."

He stopped pulling and frowned at her, trying not to notice the way the bodice of her gown clung to her ample breasts. "Jasper spoke with you today? Christ, don't tell me it was about what happened in the bleeding library this morning."

"Actually, it was about what happened with Lord Gregson," she said, worry in her tone and warm brown gaze.

The mere mentioning of the bastard's name had him longing to whip the whoreson again.

"What of 'im? Jasper ain't the sort of chap to take a cove who forced himself on a lady lightly." Indeed, if he knew his brother, Jasper had likely found the viscount himself and exacted his own retribution. "If he somehow discovered what happened to you when you were in Lord Landsdowne's employ, I promise he ain't going to hold it against you."

She shook her head, and he realized that her hair was demurely hidden beneath an ugly cap. His fingers itched to pluck it off to allow the radiance of her hair to shine in the candlelight. But that would be foolish indeed.

He was already tempted enough.

"It is not about what happened to me," she clarified softly, her countenance growing more concerned. "It is about what happened to Lord Gregson. Apparently, he was able to discover I am now in the employ of your brother's household. He went to The Sinner's Palace quite irate over what had befallen him in my name."

The whipping he had received.

"Fuck," Rafe muttered.

He could have kicked himself in the arse for invoking Persephone's name. The only reason he had done so was because he had wanted Viscount Gregson to be bloody sure the reason he had received such a basting was because of what he had done to her. What he had tried to do to her. And to make certain he would think twice before ever attempting to force himself upon another innocent sharing his roof, a woman without the power to refuse him.

Belatedly, he realized Persephone's cheeks were pink. He reckoned gentlemen didn't use oaths in the presence of ladies where she came from. And then he wondered just where it was that she came from.

"Forgive me," he said, with great feeling. "For the crudeness of my language and for any trouble I invited. If the bastard dares to return to The Sinner's Palace making demands, I'll whip 'im again."

He meant those words. Lord how he meant them.

"Thank you, but I do not think it shall be necessary." Persephone frowned. "At least I hope it shall not be."

"Gregson ain't going to cause any more problems for you, Persephone," he vowed. "I won't allow it."

The fierce protectiveness he felt toward her was troubling, but like the sky above him and the sun rising every morning on a new day, it was simply there. Beyond his control.

"I have no wish to cause you any problems, either with your brother or at your gaming hell," she said softly. "Mr. Sutton asked me about the morning Anne and Elizabeth came to my room and you told them I was sleeping. He told me he made some inquiries concerning what happened to Lord Gregson. I...I believe he may suspect you were involved."

It was possible. Jasper knew Sophie too. Their circles hadn't always been so damned lofty as they had now become, what with Jasper marrying into the quality.

"You won't cause me problems, lovely," he reassured Persephone, hating how fretful and tense she appeared, hating that Gregson could still affect her. "Don't worry your pretty head about it."

The urge to take her in his arms and kiss away that frown was stronger than the need to take another breath. He banished it by sheer force of will.

"I thought you should know, should Mr. Sutton wish to speak with you about the matter." Her brown gaze, flecked with hints of gold, seared his. "He has requested I stay away from you while you are a guest here."

"He did, did he?" That rather nettled. What did Jasper think he was going to do? Tup Miss Wren?

Well, then he supposed his brother would not have been far from the mark. *Hell.*

"Yes." Her lips compressed. "I am concerned he thinks there is more to our friendship than I admitted. You need not fear I told him about...about...what happened in the library. That is best forgotten, of course."

Something inside Rafe, already stretched dangerously thin—some thread that was the last shred of honor he possessed—snapped. Severed beneath the weight of the moment, his desire for Persephone, Jasper interfering in his life, this business with Lord Gregson, *everything*.

One moment, he was determined to keep his distance, and the next, he was reaching for her waist, drawing her body slowly into his. He was careful to give her every chance to deny him, to withdraw. But she settled against him as if it were where she was meant to be.

And it felt as if she was. How perfectly they fit together, hip to hip, breast to chest. Her mouth was only a bit below his. Lowering his head enough to seize her lips with his required scarcely any effort at all.

Her hands were on his shoulders, not pushing him away but holding on to him, her eyes wide, fringed by cinnamon-colored lashes. A trail of freckles bedecked the bridge of her dainty nose.

"You can't say it, can you?" he asked, devouring her with his gaze the way he longed to do with his lips.

"Can't say what?" Her head tipped back, and the hideous cap slid, revealing some of her glorious hair.

He caught the thing between his thumb and forefinger and plucked it from her head, tossing it to the floor. "It's a sin to cover your hair with that bleeding thing," he told her before answering her query. "You can't bring yourself to say what happened between us. That you kissed me."

A flush stole over her cheekbones, painting them pink. "I was dreadfully forward. I must beg your forgiveness for my actions."

He shook his head. "I'll not forgive you. Nor will I forget it."

"No?" Her countenance turned stricken.

"No." He gave in to temptation and kissed the tip of her nose, where those mesmerizing little flecks dotted her creamy skin like pigment shaken from an artist's brush. Her skin was smooth and warm and vital beneath his lips. He raised his head, holding her gaze. "Because I wanted you to kiss me, Persephone. And I bloody well loved it."

Her lips parted, the coal-black discs at the center of her eyes going wide. "You did?"

"Yes." He kissed her temple next, burying his nose in the curls which had burst forth to frame her face in the absence of the abysmal cap. "I want you to do it again. Now. Here."

"But I promised Mr. Sutton…"

He kissed her ear, the sweet dip behind it, smiling against her silken skin when she sighed. "To the devil with my brother. He ain't my king, and he ain't yours either."

Some part of him warned him this was foolish. That of all the terrible ideas he'd had in his years, this was by far the worst. But Persephone was in his arms, where she belonged. What would be the harm in keeping her here, just a bit longer?

He sensed the moment she surrendered to her own desires, the rigidity seeping from her body. She went pliant, her hands sliding along his shoulders to lock behind his neck. When her fingers slipped into his hair, her nails gently grazing his scalp, he could not suppress his groan.

"Your hair is so soft," she said, wonder in her voice. "I never knew a man's hair could be this silken."

According to his long-departed ma, he had been born with a head of curls, and it had never left. As a lad, it had been a bane, but when he'd been old enough to draw the eyes of the lasses, he had realized it was his glory. And then later, as a man, he'd discovered it was not his only glory. Saints be praised for that.

"I like your hands in it," he told her.

She touched him in a way no other woman had, with a hesitant admiration, as if she did not trust herself. And yet also with such tenderness, it made him ache. In his heart and lower, too.

"Have you always worn it longer than fashion?" she asked, still sifting through his hair as if it were a newly discovered treasure.

Damn, but he loved everything about the way she made him feel.

"I have always worn it as I wished, and to the devil with fashion." He grinned against her skin.

"I should return to my room," she said, but there was scarcely any intent in her voice to accompany the words.

No doubt about it, she should. She ought to run. Flee as fast as she could back to the safety of her small room. But he could not bear the thought of watching her go.

He pressed a line of kisses down her throat. "Or you could stay a little while, now that you've risked all to find your way into my chamber."

He was being reckless.

But where she was concerned, most of his good intentions had absconded.

He was consumed by his need to keep her here with him. To kiss her and pleasure her. Aye, there were ways to bring a woman to her pinnacle without tupping her. And no one would ever be the wiser. What Jasper didn't know couldn't hurt him.

"I...oh..."

He found a particularly sensitive spot on her neck and centered all his efforts there, sucking and licking and nipping her lightly with his teeth. She liked that, his prim governess. And suddenly, he would give his very life to make her come. To make her shudder and weep and know the heights of pleasure given as it should be, rather than to know the force of another's attempt to wield his physical strength over her.

"What do you say, lovely?" he asked, holding his breath as he awaited her answer.

～

What did she say?

Good heavens, what *could* she say with his lips working their magic on her? Persephone was dressed in one of her most drab gowns, and yet, her modest bodice and the dull, gray linen and mobcap had apparently done nothing to dull his ardor. His hands were on her, his kisses too. Moving, shifting all the determination she had garnered within, and she was helpless to resist him.

His words swirled through her mind, adding to the pleasurable delirium being in Rafe's presence created.

Because I wanted you to kiss me, Persephone. And I bloody well loved it.

For as long as she lived, and despite whatever came to pass in her future, these were sentences she would place in her heart and carry there forever. They would always be a part of her, as would these stolen, wicked moments with him.

She had come to his chamber this evening, knowing it would be a risk to do so and yet feeling indebted to him for his kindness to her. Mr. Sutton had been displeased, and she would no sooner cause strife for Rafe than she would herself. If Mr. Sutton wanted her to stay away from his brother, then she must honor his wishes. The alternative, losing her post, was tantamount to failure.

She would sooner die than return to Cousin Bartholomew in disgrace, so close to having won her freedom from him and yet, at the last minute, denied. But the longer she had waited for Rafe in his room, pacing the carpets and rehearsing what she must say, reminding herself she needed to inform him of his brother's suspicions and then leave, the more another, wanton part of her had wondered what would happen if she remained.

The moment he had pulled her into his embrace, bringing their bodies together, hers flush against his, his heat and strength burning into her, the wanton part of her had taken the reins. The rational, calm Persephone had disappeared, no match for the fiery sensations Rafe inspired in her.

Still, she did not know what the repercussions would be for him. It was her understanding that the Sutton siblings owned The Sinner's Palace together. However, it was possible Mr. Sutton, as the eldest of his family, owned more than the others. It was possible Rafe could be dismissed as well, or that Mr. Sutton would take other action against him.

She had to try one more time to dissuade him from his course. To dissuade them both.

"Staying here is foolish," she said on a gasp as he sucked on the tender flesh of her throat. She was breathless. Nearly mindless. She was his, whatever he wished of her. "I could be dismissed, and you..." Her words trailed away as he kissed back up her neck, not stopping until he reached her mouth.

He kissed the right corner, denying her what she craved, the full press of his lips on hers. "And you?"

He was prompting her to complete her thought. But the

impediment to doing so was that she no longer was capable of thoughts. Not rational, reasonable ones, anyway.

"Oh, Rafe," she managed, cupping his face in her hands. The slight prick of golden whiskers on his jaw was a new delight. At last, she felt its texture on her palms and the sensitive undersides of her fingers. She had been longing to feel the rasp of his whiskers from the moment she had first seen them. "Kiss me."

He kissed the opposite corner of her mouth, obeying her command but not in the way she wanted. "I'm not like the other one, you know. If you want to leave, you're free to go."

Of course she knew he was nothing like Viscount Gregson. The two men could not be more dissimilar.

"I know you are not," she reassured him, allowing her touch to trail over his cheekbones, the high, carved slashes she had only admired but never touched. "I want to be here with you, though I know it is most unwise."

His head lifted, his hazel stare meeting hers.

"You're safe with me, Persephone," he said solemnly. "Safe with me and safe from others. No one will come to my room, and I'll make certain no one sees you return to yours when you decide to go."

He sounded so confident, as if he conducted trysts every day. But then, with his sinful good looks and his confident, sensual air, perhaps he did.

She did not want to think of that now. Nor did she want to think of the others who would inevitably follow her. For this stolen moment, he was hers, and she was his. The scars of the past and the uncertainties of the future could not find them here.

"I do feel safe with you," she reassured him, touched by his need to be sure she felt no danger.

"You didn't always," he reminded her wryly, still searching

her eyes, as if they possessed all the answers he sought. "You drugged me."

Guilt lanced her. "It was not you. It was never you. It was merely my own desperation and fears."

He nodded, his jaw tensing beneath her fingers. "If you want to stop, tell me. If you don't want this, say it now. You're in control."

She nodded, grateful that he understood so well what she needed. Perhaps better, even, than she knew herself. She was in control, he had said. Which meant she did not need to wait for him to kiss her.

They were almost the same height. All she needed to do was roll to the balls of her feet and press her mouth to his. He responded immediately, his lips moving against hers, hungry and demanding and hot.

So hot.

She came to life, opening for his questing tongue. He tasted of spirits and sin and something indefinably heady. *Him.* Rafe. He may have told her she was in control, but she had lost all ability to rein in her body. Her arms wound around his neck, and she aligned herself shamelessly to him, seeking, searching.

This was what had been missing from her life. This man, this feeling.

The kiss went on, and she gave herself to it fully, just as she intended to give herself to him.

Give herself to him?

Yes! Why had the thought not occurred to her earlier?

The realization struck her like a knell of sudden clarity. A lady was told all her life that her worth was in her virtue. That she must guard and preserve it at all costs. What if she had none?

If Cousin Bartholomew were to find her tomorrow, no longer the virginal miss he had been determined to claim for his own, would he stomach the prospect of forcing her into marriage? The answer was elusive, but she felt quite certain it would, at the very least, prove an appalling discovery to him. And if he were indeed to discover her before she reached five-and-twenty, at least she would have this memory to cling to.

Persephone was justifying her shamelessness, but there was no longer a need for that when Rafe's knowing fingers found the ties of her gown and undid them. Her bodice sagged. Fabric pooled down her arms. And still he kissed her, devouring her with lips, tongue, and teeth.

Her gown fell to the floor, leaving her feeling curiously light. She wore only her shift, stays, petticoats, and stockings. His fingers slipped into her simple coiffure, pulling all the pins and dismantling her morning efforts. His lips moved over hers, coaxing the response he wanted, the low growl in his throat gratifying. To think, this handsome, seductive man wanted her. Persephone Wren, a drab governess who had done everything she could to blend in with her surroundings.

He wanted her without knowing who she was. He wanted her, not the power he had over her, not her inheritance, nothing but what she would willingly surrender. How strong and beautiful he made her feel. She told him with her kiss, her tongue mating with his as her fingers sifted through his soft curls and then traveled lower.

To the knot of his cravat. Removing their outer layers seemed both symbolic and necessary. She wanted all the barriers gone, longed for him as he had been the night he had spent in her bed, all bare, masculine flesh, sinew and muscle. The knot came undone, and blindly, she moved to the buttons of his waistcoat, fingers gliding over silk, plucking each one from its moorings.

He shrugged it and his coat from his shoulders.

But when she moved to the short row of buttons at the neck of his shirt, he broke the kiss, stepping back. She knew a pang of disappointment along with a rush of embarrassment. Had she mistook his intentions?

"Have I displeased you?" she asked, searching his gaze, her lips still tingling from his passionate kisses.

"Never, lovely." He kissed the tip of her nose. "You please me far too much. I don't trust myself to remove all. The rest of my articles must stay on."

"But—"

He silenced her protest with a swift, maddening kiss.

By the time their lips parted, she forgot what her objection was. With the practiced ease of a lady's maid, he stripped her of her undergarments. Tapes and knots could not deter him from what he wanted. From *her*. Until at last, she stood in only a shift and stockings. And then, one more sweet, slow kiss, and even the shift was gone. She stood before him in nothing but her stockings, the plain garters tied above her knees.

Naked as she had never been before another. The cool air of the chamber swirled around her, but she was warm. Warmer still when he stepped back to look at her. Beneath his admiring gaze, she felt lovely for the first time. She felt worthy of that admiration, and more than that, she reveled in it.

His hazel stare traveled over her with undisguised hunger. "You are so bleeding beautiful, Persephone. Christ. I could look upon you all day."

She pressed her thighs together to quell the ache, wishing he were as bereft of garments as she was. "Thank you."

He held out his hand to her. "Come."

She placed her palm in his, their fingers intertwining, with the wild, impulsive thought that she would follow him anywhere he wished flashing through her mind. He led her to the bed instead, which was much larger and more ornate than hers, befitting the guest chamber of such an impressive town house. Her heart sped. The bed was his. He had lain in it. She was going to lie there with him.

It will not be the first time, Persephone.

Yes, she had shared a bed with him before. But he had been snoring, and she had built a wall of pillows and coverlets to protect her. This was different. Quite different. She knew him now. She trusted him now.

They stopped just short of the mattress, and he drew her against him, kissing her lingeringly until the desire overtook her tension. She felt achy in strange new places, her nipples hardened, the flesh between her thighs throbbing. He dragged his lips down her throat to the place where her shoulder and neck met, then over her shoulder blade where he lightly bit.

Her knees went weak, but Rafe's arm banded around her waist, catching her and keeping her from falling. Slowly, tenderly, he guided her to the bed, and then she was on her back, with his big, strong body atop hers.

The desire dissipated once more, chased by the unwanted remembrance of the night Lord Gregson had come to her room at Lord Landsdowne's town house. The bedclothes had been twisted about her ankles, and he had used his upper body to pin her to the mattress, denying her the ability to escape.

This is not Gregson. This is Rafe. You are safe with Rafe.

But no matter how many times she repeated the reassurance to herself, the panic was rising within, swiftly and uncontrollably. Her body and mind were at war, wanting and yet fearful. She stiffened, going cold, the memories of that awful night chasing her passions and leaving her like the ashes in a grate after the fire had burned out.

Rafe's face rose over hers, concern lining his handsome countenance. "What's wrong, sweet?"

Her chest was suddenly heaving, tremors shaking through her. Her voice failed Persephone. It was as if she had no power to stop this sudden dread threatening to overwhelm her.

He rolled to his side, his weight lifting from her, and she could breathe again. Gradually, the alarm subsided, her heart slowing. She drew air into her lungs, staring at the plasterwork on the ceiling above them, trying to gather her wits.

Tenderly, he stroked her cheek. "Have I frightened you? Do you wish to stop? Talk to me, Persephone."

He was so much more than she had supposed he was that fateful night of their first meeting. Such a complex and caring man, one who championed her and touched her with such gentle reverence, but yet could inflict vengeance and pain upon others with the same hands that caressed her. She had only to look into his eyes to calm, to understand she was in no harm. To return to her senses.

Words accompanied the lucidity.

"When I awoke that night, he was atop me," she struggled to explain. "It... For a fleeting moment, all I could think about was Lord Gregson holding me in place, and I... I panicked. Forgive me, Rafe."

Tears stung her eyes. Tears of frustration and humiliation. She wanted Rafe Sutton more than she had ever wanted anything, aside from her freedom. And yet, why could she not escape the damage Lord Gregson had done to her? She had ruined everything.

Or perhaps, to be more accurate, *she* was ruined.

"Hush." He kissed her forehead. "There is nothing to forgive. Christ, I should be begging your forgiveness. With what that bastard did to you, I never should've touched you."

"No." She seized his shoulders, frantic, fearing he would leave the bed. "Please. I want you, Rafe."

And she did.

She could overcome the fear, she was sure. She could overpower her body, those terrible memories.

"Maybe you aren't ready, lovely." His gaze was warm, soft with understanding. "You've been through a hellish scrape."

"I *am* ready." At least, her heart and her mind were.

He leaned into her, careful to keep his body from pressing against her, his lips finding hers. It was what she needed, the seductive governing of his mouth slanting on hers, calming her, bringing her back to the reason she was here. This man. His kisses. The way he made her feel.

Lovely.

Desired.

Powerful.

Fearless.

As if there were no troubles in her world, everything in its proper order. As if she had no need to fear the future, the coming day. All was right when Rafe Sutton kissed her.

He ended the connection, pulling back to study her with an intensity that made her skin prickle with awareness. She could not shake the sense he was delving into her, finding a part of her she had not previously known existed. Seeing all her secrets. Which was foolish, of course. He could not see the truth. He was not omniscient. He was merely a man.

"There will always be another day," he said, breaking the silence.

But that was the trouble. For her, there was every possibility there would not. On another day, she would lose her daring. Or he would have found another woman to ply with his charms. Or Mr. Sutton would finally uncover the entire truth about her and dismiss her. Mayhap Cousin Bartholomew would find her and force her to return to

Silwood Manor. A myriad of possibilities, of lost chances. She could not bear to let him go without at least trying once more.

"What if there is not another day?" She swallowed hard against a swelling tide of emotion, trying in vain to read his expression. "What if this is our only chance, Rafe? If there will never be another night when we can be so free?"

That fear, more than the terror which beset her whenever she was reminded of the day Lord Gregson had nearly forced himself upon her, spurred her the most. If she was forced to marry Cousin Bartholomew, or if she spent the rest of her life as a governess, or even if she was able to free herself from her cousin's plans and live out her life as a spinster, she wanted more. She wanted the memory of having known passion, real and true, once in her life.

He kissed her again, so softly it was little more than a whisper of a touch, his lips feathering over hers before it ended. "Is it my body on yours that sparked your fears?"

She nodded, biting her lip. "Yes. I do think so."

He kissed her brow. "I can pleasure you without being atop you, sweet. Do you want to try?"

Heavens and angels, did he need to ask?

"Yes." In her relief, she leaned forward, kissing him so hard that her teeth slammed into the sensitive insides of her lips. But never mind. She did not care.

He broke the kiss and rolled to his back. "Come here, lovely."

He offered her his hand once more.

And she took it.

CHAPTER 9

*W*hat he was about to do was not the sort of thing a man attempted with an innocent. And yet, in this instance, it was a necessity. That rank, chicken-hearted scoundrel had hurt her, and unlike a physical lashing, the scars dwelled beneath the surface. Now, it was for Rafe to undo the damage as best he could.

Giving Persephone pleasure was a start.

Not that his motives were entirely pure. Pleasing her would also please him. Very much.

He lay on his back and guided her legs until she was astride his chest. All the saints, what a glorious sight to behold. Persephone was naked save her stockings and garters, creamy thighs parted to reveal the pretty pink bud between her lips, the thatch of sunset curls on her mound not enough to shield the slick pink folds from view. He caressed her hips, aware she was nervous and embarrassed to be displayed for him thus. The scent of her, musky and rich with desire, made his mouth water.

He was desperate to taste her. To suck her and fuck her

with his tongue until she screamed. His cock had never been harder in his life. But it would have to wait.

"Beautiful," he praised, palms gliding over the soft inner flesh of her thighs, as he allowed his gaze to travel the luscious curves of her waist, the generous handfuls of her breasts. "How do you feel?"

"Shy," she admitted, her tongue darting over the seam of her lips. "This is terribly wicked."

He was capable of far greater depravity, but no need to mention that now. Her nipples were puckered and hard, her face flush with desire. What a delicious combination she was, equal parts the prim governess and lusty wanton, the innocent and the seductress all at once.

"Never be shy with me," he told her. "I want you bold and daring and brave. Give me your wickedest."

He moved his touch nearer to her center, thumbs dipping into the creases on the edges of her plump lips. Her quim beckoned, open, wet, ready for his tongue. She shifted, sliding her arse forward in an instinctive effort to achieve more of his touch. He was unable to resist swiping his thumbs over the outer folds, gathering some of her wetness and painting it over her flesh.

"Oh," she said softly, part moan, part exclamation of wonder. She rocked forward, arching her back.

Her breasts were thrust forward, offerings he could not refuse.

He shifted her. Using his upper body's strength, he sat up, careful to keep his hands on her, his thumbs tantalizing her by lingering on the periphery of where her body would naturally want him most. He latched on to a nipple, sucking hard while he continued to tease her, and was rewarded by her soft sound of delight and her fingers threading through his hair.

There's my girl.

His? Yes. Hell yes. No time to question the possessive way he felt about Miss Persephone Wren now. For tonight, these precious, stolen hours, she *was* his. And she was naked, on him, her cunny soaking the thin fabric of his shirt. He had never known a more erotic moment in his life when he still had his bleeding togs on.

He sucked her other nipple, then caught it in his teeth and tugged. The need to take his time with her and drive her to the edge of madness was equally as strong as the urge to haul her cunny to his face and sink his tongue deep. Only when the muscles in his abdomen began to quake beneath the strain did he relent, resuming his supine position.

She was flushed, her breath coming in fast gasps that showed him she was as affected as he was. Good. But there was more, far more, to come. He massaged the dip between her inner thighs and her mound, running his thumbs up and down her seam to gather more moisture.

She squirmed, a helpless mewl slipping from her lips.

Rafe was greedy where Persephone was concerned, and he could not be sure if he wanted her to come from his fingers or his mouth first.

He licked his lips, attempting to repress the desperation and prolong the moment. "Have you ever touched yourself before, sweet?"

Her befuddled expression sank talons into his heart. "Of course I touch myself when I bathe or dress."

He suppressed a groan at her innocence, the gleaming possibility *he* could be the one to show her pleasure. "Not in that sense. Have you ever touched yourself here?" As he posed the question, he ran his thumbs to the top of her mound, illustrating his point. One thumb gently lifted her soft, warm wetness to reveal her pearl more fully. The other caressed the length of her. "Here, love. Have you ever stroked yourself here, where you are so deliciously sensitive?"

She inhaled as he gave her swollen nub another swipe. Her hips jerked, bringing her nearer to his face. "Yes."

Her hissed admission made his ballocks draw tight and his cock ache with almost painful pleasure. His seed was already seeping from the tip, moistening the linen that rubbed against his cock head in a maddening abrasion with each pump of his own hips. If he was not careful, he was going to spend in his bloody smalls.

"How do you touch yourself?" he asked. "Lightly?" He demonstrated, giving her a light stroke, then a soft, lazy swirl. "Slowly?"

"Mmm," was all she said.

"Faster?" he asked, brushing over the sweetly engorged bud from left to right, his thumb moving swiftly.

She made another sound and her hips jerked, giving him all the answer he needed.

"Yes, lovely." He pressed harder as he continued at a faster pace. "This is how you like it, aye?"

She leaned forward, planting her hands on the headboard behind him, the globes of her breasts dangling temptingly near to his mouth. She was panting, gasping, straining against him, and he had not even licked her yet. *Good.* He would make her spend with his fingers first. And then when she was sensitive and wet and throbbing, he would use his tongue.

"This is your pearl, sweet," he told her, flattening the heel of his palm on her mound to apply more pressure and rubbing at a furious pace. "How does it feel when I touch you this way?"

Her hips were seeking, body bowing, skin flushing with the glow of her pleasure. A woman was the only instrument Rafe had ever learned to play, and he was glad of it now. How badly he wanted to sink his fingers into her cunny, to breach her, to feel her tight heat clamping around him and drawing him in.

Her only answer was a moan. But he wanted more. He wanted words. Needed her admission so that long after this night, he could recall what it had felt like to hear this starchy sunset-haired governess tell him she liked the way he fucked her.

"Tell me, Persephone," he said, using her given name and his most commanding voice. "Tell me if you like my hand on your cunny."

Her gaze, heavy-lidded with desire, met his. "I do. You feel wondrous."

Although she had given him what he wanted—her admission that she liked what he was doing to her—she had not given him the satisfaction of using a bawdy word. He wanted to hear her demure voice saying the word *cunny*.

"That ain't what I asked for," he said, removing his hand even as she writhed. Instead, he painted the inside of her thigh with her own wetness, drawing tantalizingly close to her drenched center without touching the glistening flesh. "Say it the way I did. Tell me you like my hand on your cunny." He leaned up and sucked her nipple, then gently bit before withdrawing to blow hot air over the straining tip. "Give me the words and I'll make you come."

He wondered if she knew what that meant, whether or not she had ever brought herself to spend. The thought of Persephone lying alone in her bed, those dainty fingers working between her thighs, was enough to make him groan.

"I love your hand on my cunny, Rafe," she said then, her tone gone husky with need. "Please, do not stop."

Ah, hell. Sometimes, a man asked for a gift he could not bear receiving. This was one such gift. Because now, he would never be able to forget, for as long as he lived, the sound of Persephone Wren's dulcet voice telling him she loved his hand on her cunny.

"Good lass," he praised, kissing the side of her other breast as he cupped her hot center and resumed his effort to make her spend. "You are so pretty and pink and wet here for me."

She moaned and pumped her hips into his hand. He worked her harder, flicking his tongue over the stiff peak of her breast. Faster. She was impossibly slick, hot and throbbing beneath his fingers. And then, she was stiffening, crying out. Shuddering as her release hit her. He showed her no quarter, determined to wring every bit of pleasure from her, plumping her clitoris with his thumb as she shook and moaned. With her sensitivity heightened, he knew the act was painfully pleasurable. But he wanted to keep her on the edge.

"I want to taste you, sweet," he said. "I want to lick up every drop of your spend and then fuck you with my tongue."

"Oh dear heavens," she said, sounding dazed and half-wild. "Yes. Please."

He released her breast, his own desperation seizing him, and his head dropped to the pillow as he caught her bottom in his hands and pulled her the rest of the way, until her thighs rested on either side of his face and her dripping cunny was his to feast on.

And feast he did, doing his utmost to control the wild impulse to suck and bite and otherwise make her his. This was Persephone, and he could not recall ever wanting a woman as much. But he needed to go slowly. To listen to her cues even when all he wanted to do was devour her until she screamed.

He licked along her seam, gathering all her wetness and the taste of her exploded in his senses. More delicious than he could have imagined. Musk and flowers and something else that was purely Persephone. He groaned into her cunny, still gripping her rump, angling her over his face so he could latch on to her pearl. She was already swollen and slick everywhere, but most especially here, and whether it was his lust rendering him dicked in the nob or it was real, he swore she pulsed on his tongue.

He sucked hard, and she made a low sound of approval, rocking herself into his face in encouragement. So he sucked harder, then feathered his tongue over her in teasing, light strokes.

"Rafe."

His name was a moan escaping her. Christ, he would never forget the way she sounded, drunk with lust while she rode his mouth. He kneaded her arse cheeks as he licked and sucked, the hushed sounds of her appreciation growing louder with each stroke of his tongue.

This was a dangerous game they played. He could not afford to be caught, and nor could she. Yet, he forgot to care with her demanding cunny thrusting against him. His tongue traveled along her outer lips, then parted her folds, dipping shallowly into her. She was impossibly hot there, and smooth and wet. Her juices were dribbling down his chin, and he hoped he would smell her on himself in the morning when he woke, naked and alone in this same bed.

And what a bloody shame that would be, waking in this bed without her.

It was necessary, however. They were not meant for more than this stolen night. This shared passion and pleasure. Holding to that thought, he licked up her seam and suckled her clitoris once more. She cried out, her thighs stiffening and closing around his head. Undulating against him, she came fiercely, collapsing partially against him, rhythmically thrusting, seeking more.

But this was still not enough for Rafe. If he only had tonight, he wanted to sate her so thoroughly, there would never be another who could match the heights he had shown her. Years from now, he wanted her to remember Rafe Sutton's mouth bringing her to her peak until she was limp and mindless.

Determined, he licked into her again, long, probing swipes of his tongue over her quivering flesh.

"Rafe, please."

Oh, yes. His insatiable little governess wanted more. She writhed against him, her fingers somehow having found their way back to his hair, twisting in the long locks and pulling as she fucked his face. This position had been meant to allay the fears and painful memories dogging her, but now she was truly the one in control, taking what she wanted, demanding he lick and suck her until she spent again.

It was too delicious, and he was on the edge himself. Using his teeth, he nibbled on her pearl, finding a place where she was especially sensitive and her cries turned to mewls. Face buried in her cunny, he managed to open his eyes to the magnificent sight of her, hair unbound and running down her back, nipples hard and pink, breasts full, pale mounds bouncing with each erotic thrust she made.

She was wild.

And he loved it.

And he loved...

He loved...

Well, bleeding hell and all the saints, he loved *her*.

Impossible, improbable, a state he had never reckoned he would find himself in—he, Rafe Sutton, dedicated rogue and pursuer of petticoats. It made no sense, and it was terrifying, and yet, it simply was.

Ah, what a time to make this bleeding revelation. Strangely, it did nothing to quell his ardor. If anything, the knowledge made him harder. Made his ability to suppress the crashing wave of his release impossible. His right hand released his hold on her rump and traveled the familiar path to his cock. No time to remove it from his trousers and smalls. Instead, he pressed his palm beneath the thick ridge, jerking upward in a rude approximation of screwing. Not nearly as good as his hand on his bare cock and nowhere near the heaven it would be to sink deep inside Persephone's sweet cunny, but it would have to suffice.

He raked his teeth over her pearl as she moaned and thrusted, as his hand passed over his cock, desperate for relief and hungry enough that not even two layers of fabric could hinder the sensation. Then he sucked. He sucked hard on that greedy nub, until with his left hand, he shifted her so that once more his tongue dipped into her, and he sucked her lips and cunny, drinking her dew as if it were manna from heaven sent. Her sounds above him told him she was about to reach another release.

She was begging.

And he was lost.

He gave her everything he had, licking, sucking, using his teeth and tongue and lips. His jaw ached, and still he ate her until she came undone with a muffled scream. She shuddered and quivered and collapsed against the headboard with such abandon, the dull thud of her head striking the wood rang through the room. One hard press of his hand to his cock, and he exploded too, coming so violently, there was a moment of physical pain arcing across his chest, potent and powerful and oddly enjoyable, this sign that he had just come harder than he ever had before.

As the waves of bliss washed over him, he held her there, gentling his mouth on her, absorbing the throbs and spasms of her, understanding he would never know another night like this.

Persephone was jarred awake by a knocking on her door.

Blinking, she rolled over, feeling terribly lazy and wonderfully delicious, body humming with awareness in delightful new places, and…

Awareness and lucidity returned in a jolt. Her eyes cast wildly around the chamber, which was lit by the risen sun beyond the curtains.

Dear heavens!

This was not her room.

She was in a guest room.

Rafe's room, to be specific.

And he was at her side, sleeping soundly, looking like a sinful angel in repose, still dressed in his shirt, the bedclothes tangled about his waist. While she was—a quick glance beneath the counterpane confirmed her fears—naked save for the stockings and garters she had never removed.

She had slept here.

And now, someone was knocking on Rafe's door.

"Damn it, Rafe, wake up," called the irate voice on the other side of the portal.

She gasped, recognizing that voice too well. At her side Rafe stirred, coming to with a start. He blinked, looking unfairly handsome for such a dire situation. His brow furrowed for a moment as his gaze met hers, and then a slow grin spread on his sensual lips, as if he were recalling what had passed between them the night before.

Thump, thump, thump.

"Rafe, you bloody arse!" In the hall, Mr. Sutton was growing angrier.

The moment was effectively severed.

"Jasper!" Rafe shot up, alarm in his expression. "What the devil?"

Persephone was certain he was going to demand to know whether or not she was within the room. She braced herself, tensing, a rush of shame hitting her with such sudden ferocity, her eyes burned.

Why had she allowed herself to remain for a few minutes in the wake of their explosive passion the night before? Why had she fallen asleep instead of returning to her own room? Now, she would be discovered, and despite the East End origins of Jasper Sutton, she knew there was no way he would allow her to remain on as governess after she had been cavorting with his brother.

Just as it was for a lady, the reputation was paramount to a governess. Maintaining one's virtue was a necessity.

"We have a problem at The Sinner's Palace," Mr. Sutton said curtly, cutting through her fears. "The Bradleys are causing trouble again, and I need you to accompany me. Get your arse out of bed, you bleeding tosspot. We haven't time to waste."

"Sodding Bradleys," Rafe muttered, running his fingers through his curls and leaving them charmingly disheveled. Louder, he called, "I'll be out in a trice."

"I'm waiting," Mr. Sutton announced, his voice grim.

"Let a man take his morning piss in peace, will you?" Rafe shouted back. "I'll meet you in the mews in ten minutes."

She would have flushed at his candor, but she was naked in his bed, and his tongue had been on her most intimate flesh. It was rather too late for her to be shocked.

"I'll give you five, and then I'll haul your arse out myself," Mr. Sutton warned.

"Fine," Rafe agreed, tossing back the bedclothes and rising.

She watched, too afraid to speak, as he stalked across the room and pressed his ear to the door. Her heart was pounding as fast as it had last night. She pressed a trembling hand to it, holding the counterpane over her bare breasts as if it were a shield.

What manner of scrape have you managed to find yourself in now, Persephone? So close to reaching your majority, and you have fallen into bed with a seductive rogue and courted scandal and ruin.

Rafe turned back to her. "Jasper's gone now. We need to get you dressed and back to your room before anyone sees you."

The return to her own chamber loomed. It was not far, and yet it may as well have been on another continent. So many chances for discovery.

She wetted her suddenly dry lips. "You needn't worry over me. Your brother is awaiting you. I will find my way to my rooms."

"That ain't the way of it, lovely." He strode toward her, frowning, and perhaps it was wrong of her, but she found her gaze lingering on his mouth.

Heavens, what his mouth had done to her. She was shameless, because despite the danger of her carefully constructed walls of lies crumbling around her, the place between her legs thrummed. She pressed her thighs together beneath the bedclothes to subdue the ache, but it only served to heighten the sensation and make her aware she was shockingly wet.

What had happened to her?

Rafe Sutton.

He was what had happened to her. This dangerous, glorious, caring, sweet, passionate man. And now she was not just in danger of losing her position, but her heart as well.

"I'll be seeing you back safely where you belong," he said sternly, arriving at the side of her bed with an armful of her discarded garments from the night before. "Come now, we've got to get you dressed."

She had been so caught up in her own musings that she had failed to note him gathering her gown and petticoats. But although she had been quite free with her nudity last evening, and despite the intimacies they had shared, she found herself strangely reluctant to slip from his bed naked by the harsh light of morning.

"Shy?" Rafe asked, his tone so tender she could have wept. "No need for that, lovely. Shall I turn my back?"

He was acting as if Mr. Sutton had not put a time constraint on his appearance. As if the household would not be bustling about when they exited the room. As if nothing they had done was wrong. And she was grateful for it. His easy manner helped her panic to calm.

"Surely you do not intend to help me dress," she said. "I can do that myself. I have been for some time now."

Drat. She was once more revealing far too much. But if Rafe found anything to question in her words, he was saving it for another occasion.

Instead, he gave her a grin that showed his dimples. "You don't need to dress yourself with me about. I'm a dab hand with a lady's buntlings."

The reminder that he likely had a vast number of women awaiting his attentions made a fierce surge of jealousy curdle her stomach. To her mortification, she realized she did not want this man to ever touch another lady's *buntlings*, whatever they were. Only hers.

It is not meant to be, Persephone.

But what if it was?

Her heart ached.

"If you must," she said.

"I must."

She allowed him to draw her from the bed. His efficient motions made it clear this was no seduction. Her shift went over her head, and he smoothed it over her sides and hips before attending to her stays and petticoat. Her gown was last.

"Turn."

She did as he asked, and he tied her tapes, then worked his magic on her hair, sifting his fingers through the tangled locks. Surely he did not intend to dress her unruly red curls as well, did he?

Before she could ask or even protest, he was winding it into a coil. Hair pins gently raked her scalp as he slid them into place.

"There we are." His breath was hot on her nape as his hands settled on her shoulders.

She shivered, wondering if he would set his lips there, fearing she could not control herself if he did. But then, Rafe spun her about so that she faced him once more.

His expression was as tender as his touch had been. "I ain't going to be hired as a lady's maid any time soon, but you'll do."

Her fingers flew to her hair, tentatively inspecting his work. It seemed he was indeed adept at dressing a lady's hair as well. Once again, the thought of the ladies on whom he had previously practiced made a possessive bolt of envy dash through her.

"Thank you," she said shakily. "Have you seen my cap?"

"It's a sin to cover your hair with that abomination."

"Where is it?" she asked, undeterred.

"I tossed it into the fire last night." His grin was unrepentant.

And slightly triumphant.

"Rafe! You cannot burn my caps. I only have three."

"Two." He kissed the tip of her nose. "We'd best 'urry, lovely. Time ain't exactly our bosom friend this morning."

"Yes," she agreed, knowing they had to part and yet somehow dreading it as well.

Because this was all they were to have.

"Come," he said offering her his hand.

"You are dressed in shirtsleeves and trousers and stockinged feet," she pointed out. "Surely Mr. Sutton will take note."

"No time for me." He took her hand in his and brought it to his lips for a kiss. "I'll 'andle Jasper. Come now. We've a room to secret you back to."

CHAPTER 10

"*Y*ou look like you spent the night rolling about the floor of The Garden of Flora, with half a dozen wenches," Jasper observed when Rafe folded his frame into the carriage bench opposite his. "Were you carousing until dawn?"

Rafe tamped down a rise of inconvenient self-loathing and gave his brother his best devil-may-give-a-scrope smile. "And what do you care what I was about? You're an old married man these days, firmly caught in the leg-shackle."

"Happily so," his brother agreed, his countenance stern. "Mayhap I want the same for my rakehell brother."

"I ain't a rakehell." He adjusted the fit of his hat on his head, frowning as he thought of what he had done.

He'd taken what Persephone offered.

Given her pleasure.

She was still a bleeding virgin.

Yes, but she was an innocent, you fucking clod pate. You could have exercised some restraint. At the very least, you should have seen her back to her room last night instead of embarking on a furtive dash through the halls this morning.

Aye, it was true. They had narrowly avoided detection. It was not an exercise in stupidity he wished to repeat.

"And next you'll tell me the sky ain't blue and the Bradleys didn't steal our latest shipment of jackey and set rats loose in The Sinner's Palace."

Christ. So that was why Jasper had summoned him. The Bradleys were waging war once more.

"Bloody bastards." Rafe's hands clenched into fists he longed to slam into the teeth of one of the Bradley lads. Or their arsehole of a sire, for that matter. "Those shit sacks are determined to ruin us one way or another. If the last basting we gave them ain't enough to get through their thick sconces, we'll just 'ave to give them another."

"First we have to make certain the rat catchers gather all the vermin," Jasper said grimly.

What a coil. And Rafe could not help but to feel responsible for it. Leaving Hart and Wolf to fend for the gaming hell and look after Lily and Pen had likely been a bad halfpenny. Wolf and Hart were capable, but Pen was a bloody handful, and Lily was still young and wild. To say nothing of the daily running of the hell.

"I ought to be staying there." Rafe shook his head. "If I'd been at The Sinner's Palace, no rats or Bradleys would've found their way past me."

"The same could be said for me," his brother acknowledged. "It ain't about whose fault this is, Rafe. It's about what we do next to clean up the mess and make damn sure it never 'appens again."

"Ever the wise brother," he grumbled, and not without a hint of bitterness.

As the eldest of the Suttons, Jasper was their leader. There had been a time when he, too, had been full of hellfire, drinking and wenching far too much. But that had very much changed in recent years, and when his twin daughters from a past tryst had come into his life, he had grown more responsible and staid, committed to Lady Octavia and Anne and Elizabeth and their welfare in the same way he had once minded the hell.

Rafe, meanwhile, had not only shirked his duties at The Sinner's Palace, but he had made a muck of his own affairs as well. He had all but shagged his nieces' governess the night before.

And he had fallen in love with her.

What to do with this information?

Last night, he thought he had been drunk on quim, the notion occurring to him because all the blood in his body had diverted to his cock. But the feelings were still there, a strangeness in the pit of his belly, a pulling in his heart, as if there were an invisible string tying him to her.

Which was ridiculous, of course. Rafe Sutton did not lose his heart to a set of petticoats. And he had known more than his fair share. He kissed them and pleased them, worshiped their bodies and charmed them and laughed with them until they parted ways. He had never, in all his days, wanted one woman to be the first sight he beheld each morning when he rose and the last he saw every night before slumber claimed him.

Until *her*.

"Anything rattling about in that knowledge box of yours?"

Jasper's voice sliced through his musings, reminding him that he was in a carriage with his brother, on his way to the East End.

To where he bloody well belonged. He had been born in the rookeries. In a large sense, it was all he knew. A man could earn coin, acquire an education, purchase the togs of a fancy cove, hang his arse over a chamber pot in Mayfair, but he would never be a lord. He would never truly rise above his station. And he would do well to remember that.

Rafe shook the knowledge box in question. "Only a few puffs of dust and some wood shavings."

Jasper snorted. "Giving yourself a fat lot of credit, aren't you? More like nothing but dust. Christ knows that any man with a brain between his ears wouldn't whip the son of an earl in a bawdy house and expect the act to go unnoticed."

Well, hell. He stiffened, searching his brother's stare, so like his own. Wondering just how much Jasper knew.

"Who would do something so bleeding stupid?" he blustered, hoping they might at least leave Persephone out of it.

But he was not to be so fortunate.

"You," his brother said coolly. "That's who. Miss Wren spun some pretty lies on your behalf, but I'm not stupid, Rafe. There's something between the two of you, and I want to know what it is and why you whipped Lord Gregson at The Garden of Flora on her behalf."

The fury, burning deep inside him from the moment Persephone had unburdened herself to him in this very conveyance, rose. It would not be contained. The story was not his to tell, but he could not sit here in silence and allow his brother to suppose the viscount an innocent man.

"Because he tried to rape her," Rafe spat. "It 'appened at her last post, and she left without a letter of character just to escape the bleeding dunghill. You must know I'd never attack a lord without cause."

Indeed, lords were who filled their purses. The Sutton family business was keeping the quality happy, not inflicting pain and humiliation upon them. The whipping had been a necessity with Gregson, however. The man deserved punishment. He deserved *more* than what he had got.

"Hell," Jasper swore fiercely, his countenance going dark with the same rage coursing through Rafe's veins. Suttons protected their women. "Little wonder she forged the letter from the earl. I had wondered at the reason."

"Yes." Rafe exhaled in a rush, unclenching his fists and then digging his fingers into his thighs with painful pressure. "She didn't deserve what happened to her."

His brother's ire was still tangible, his face hard as granite. "Gregson will be turned away from The Sinner's Palace and all other establishments where we assert any hint of influence. I'll also be sharing this news with Lady Octavia. The right article in her scandal journal when the first edition is released, and he'll be ruined just as he deserves."

Jasper's wife, Lady Octavia, had recently begun *Tales About Town*, a new venture that thrived on the foibles of the *ton*. Rafe would dearly love to see an article printed in its pages revealing Gregson for who and what he was.

He nodded jerkily, emotion making his throat feel thick, the words more difficult to find. "I've no doubt Persephone would like that."

He realized his mistake the moment Jasper's brows rose.

"Persephone, is it?" He shook his head. "Damn it, Rafe, just how familiar are you with the twins' governess?"

Oh, the answers he could give.

Last night, his tongue had been in her sweet cunny and lashing her pearl while she rode his face until she came. Eh, he had a feeling Jasper wouldn't appreciate that response too much. Best to try a different one.

"Familiar enough to know she's a fine woman," he said, not wishing to harm her position in Jasper's household. She'd been deuced fretful this morning, worrying over what would happen. He hated having caused her a moment of worry with his own recklessness.

"That ain't an answer, brother," Jasper said, eyes narrowing.

Rafe grinned unrepentantly. "It's the only one you're going to get."

He would guard Persephone's honor to his dying breath.

Perhaps it was all he could give her, aside from last night's pleasure, but he owed her that much. He owed her more, but he wasn't certain what he could give her.

She was a governess.

He was an East End scoundrel.

The carriage rocked to a halt outside The Sinner's Palace. This was where he belonged. His duty was to his family, he reminded himself firmly. Not to a woman who could never be his, regardless of how he felt for her. A man could love a woman and let her go because he knew he wasn't bloody well going to be the man for her.

Couldn't he?

"Hell, Rafe. What have you been doing beneath my roof?" Jasper demanded.

A scream issued from within the gaming hell.

"Damned rats," his brother grumbled.

Rafe and Jasper scrambled from the carriage, the question left unanswered, as they hastened inside.

Three nights.

Persephone paced the carpets of her small room, trying to turn her mind to other matters and failing. It always, inevitably, returned to him.

To Rafe.

She had not seen him since the morning he had left in day-old rumpled shirtsleeves and trousers, since he had kissed her on the nose and looked at her so tenderly she must surely have imagined it all. To say nothing of the feverish passion they had shared.

Yes, she would have believed none of it had happened at all were it not for the rush of sensation that filled her—entirely new and potent and unlike anything she had ever felt before—whenever she thought about what had passed between them that night. And were it not for the memory of his frantic kisses, his knowing touch, and his big strong body at her mercy.

But it had been three nights, and still, to the best of her knowledge, he had yet to return to the house. It was possible he may never. And she was powerless to know the truth of the matter. Who could she ask? Certainly not Mr. Sutton, who already suspected something more had happened between herself and Rafe than she dared reveal. Nor Lady Octavia, and most definitely not anyone belowstairs. To do so would only cause minds to wonder and tongues to wag, and she could not afford any of those circumstances.

You are down to weeks, Persephone. A scant few weeks until you are free of Cousin Bartholomew's reign.

"Oh, heavens!" Heaving a sigh, she stalked back to the opposite end of her chamber.

The evening air held a damp chill, for it had rained all day, and not even the fire burning in her grate was sufficient to warm her. She supposed she ought to be thankful for the fireplace, at least. In her previous situation, her room had been impossibly sweltering on a warm day and numbingly cold on a chilly day. She'd never been able to amass enough bedclothes to keep herself warm. It had been one of many times when she had been forced to acknowledge the disparity between her life—one she had considered an imprisonment, of sorts—and the lives of those in service. While Cousin Bartholomew had kept her soundly beneath his thumb, she had never been physically uncomfortable.

Aside from his announcement of their betrothal and the kisses he had forced upon her. She had been eighteen then, and terribly young and untutored in all the evils which could be visited upon a girl of vast fortune with no one to protect her.

But she had been intelligent enough to understand that becoming Cousin Bartholomew's wife was not the future she wanted for herself. She had formulated her plan, and then, when the opportunity had struck, she had run.

She was *still* running. All these years later.

If he caught her now…

She shivered, refusing to allow her mind to travel to such a possibility. Cousin Bartholomew did not appreciate a challenge to his brutal authority. Nor did he approve of a woman with her own mind and will, one who did not wish to become his pawn.

"Lovely?"

On a gasp, she spun about, hand to her heart. And there he was. Not the specter of her terrified imaginings. No indeed, Cousin Bartholomew had not found her here. She could only continue to hope and pray he would not.

The man standing before her was Rafe Sutton.

Her Rafe.

Dare she think of him in such terms? She had no right. He did not know who she truly was. Her life was a massive knot of lies.

"Rafe," she said, half of her believing he was an apparition, the product of her feverish longing for him.

It had been three nights.

The longest nights of her life.

How had he managed to slip inside her room, unheard, unnoticed?

"Tell me you are not a ghost," she added, although she felt foolish the moment the words emerged.

He was near to the door, dressed in evening finery, and he could not have looked more polished and handsome if he were waltzing beneath the blazing candles of a society ball. Or, at least, she imagined he would not. Persephone had never been able to attend a true society event. Cousin

Bartholomew had made certain to keep her secluded. The air was wholesome in Oxfordshire, he had claimed, not at all thick with soot and fog as it was in London.

It had been yet another self-serving lie her guardian had told her.

Forcefully, Persephone thrust thoughts of Cousin Bartholomew from her mind. Rafe was here, and he was all she wanted to think, to know, to feel. Even if he stood somewhat hesitantly, several strides between them, he was here.

With her.

That had to account for something.

Surely?

"I ain't a ghost, sweet," Rafe said, sauntering toward her in that way he had, such pure, masculine confidence on display. "I'm damned real. Pinch me if you like."

His offer was silliness. But she did not care. Seizing upon an excuse to cut the distance between them and touch him, she moved forward. When he was within reach, she extended her right arm, her hand finding his biceps. Through the layers of his coat and shirt, his heat warmed her.

Brought her back to life.

She caught his skin and those outer layers between thumb and forefinger and did as he had suggested. Pinched. A small punishment for his absence.

"Ah!" He started, moving away from her and rubbing the place where she had touched him. "That bleeding hurt. I didn't truly intend for you to pinch me."

"Then you should not have encouraged me to do so," she countered, feeling ridiculously irritated with him now that he had finally appeared. "And nor should you have left me here for three nights, wondering where you have gone or why."

The last bit, she had meant to keep to herself. But of

course, she had blurted the words without thought. Curse her foolish tongue.

He raised a brow, considering her, lips half-quirked upward in a charming rascal's smile, the slightest hint of a dimple appearing in his left cheek. "You missed me then, did you?"

Had he thought she would not?

An unsettling thought occurred to her then. Did he ply every woman he met with such masterful pleasure? Did he make all the ladies in his acquaintance weep with the chance to have his mouth upon them once more? She wondered how many ladies were longing for him, somewhere in London, even now.

"Of course I did not," she told him, lying.

What was one more fib? Almost everything about her was a lie. Her name. Her past. Heavens, she had been someone else for so long she had forgotten what it felt like to be herself.

His countenance turned serious. "If you didn't miss me, mayhap I should go."

"No." She caught his sleeve when he would have turned away, staying his flight. "Do not go. Where have you been?"

His gaze traveled over her face, and she swore she saw hunger burning in the mysterious depths of his eyes. "Taking care of a few matters."

Belatedly, she noticed a shadow of bruising on his jaw. She reached for it, gently pressing the tips of her fingers to the mottled skin. "What happened to you?"

His grin returned. "Is that worry I hear? For me?"

Of course it was.

But she was still uncertain where she stood with him, so she withdrew her touch. "Is it not normal to be concerned for the welfare of others? One would suppose it a necessary human trait."

"Eh. Not every human has a good heart. In fact, most of them are deuced bad." He shrugged, then held up his glove-less hands for her inspection, flexing his fingers to show knuckles which were bruised and split. "But you needn't fear. The other lads had a worse time of it. I assure you of that."

"Fisticuffs?" Her ire returned. "That is what kept you away for three days?"

"That and rats. The kind with a tail and the kind without." His tone was smooth and calm, as if doing violence to others was a small matter.

Perhaps to him, it was.

She shivered. Rafe Sutton was a dangerous man.

"Cold?" He rubbed her upper arms as if to warm her. "Shall I stoke the fire?"

But how was it that she felt safe with him, despite every-thing she knew and all the warnings crowding her mind?

Because he is a good man. Because he is one of the few humans in possession of a good heart.

"Y-yes," she said, stepping away from him as she stam-mered over her words.

She was awash with confusion, longing, and something stronger. Something that felt a whole lot like...

Love.

Rafe moved away from her, prowling to the other end of the chamber where the fire had indeed begun to die. She watched as he built the flames with easy, methodical motions. Those hands were capable of so many deeds. Good and bad. They had touched her with gentle reverence. And they had also pummeled someone.

Someone deserving, as Lord Gregson had been?

"Rats, you said," she reminded him, crossing the room to avoid raising her voice too loudly. "What did you mean by that?"

Rafe was kneeling by the hearth, still tending to the fire.

She tried not to notice the way his trousers clung to his well-muscled thighs, or the suggestion of his bottom beneath the tail of his dark wool coat.

He glanced over his shoulder at her, so rakishly handsome, he stole her breath. "We've some mace coves giving us trouble at The Sinner's Palace. One of them managed to set more than a dozen rats loose inside the kitchens. They also stole some of our best bleeding booze. It had to be answered."

"With fists?" she asked.

He raised a brow. "Sometimes that's the only way, a good, sound drubbing."

His world was so very different from hers. Or, at least, from the one she had formerly inhabited, what seemed a lifetime ago.

She nodded. "I see."

He turned back to the fire, finishing tending to it. The flames were hot and high now, casting off so much warmth that it suffused her face. Then again, perhaps that was just her body's reaction to Rafe's proximity.

When he rose to his full height and turned back to her, she had to clench her fists in the skirt of her gown to keep from reaching for him.

"Warmer now?" he asked.

Too warm. And most definitely not all from the fire.

"Yes." She summoned a smile. "Thank you. Did you slip into my room merely to tend to the fire for me?"

"Of course." He offered her the same courtly bow he had given in the gardens when he had tricked Anne and Elizabeth into proving their running prowess so he could speak with her alone. "Ever at your service, milady."

When Rafe chose to charm, he was magnetic. And like before, she found herself drawn to him. Moving nearer so that she might catch a hint of his scent. To her shame, she had been seeking it in the cravat he had left the morning after she had slipped the laudanum into his brandy. It remained hidden beneath her pillow, more treasured now than it had been that first day. The scrap of linen was the only bit of him that could truly be hers, and she had no intention of parting with it.

"Why have you come here this evening?" she asked him.

He raised a brow, magnificently rakish. "I am spending the night while I tend to The Sinner's Palace II on the morrow."

"I meant to my room," she corrected softly.

"Am I not welcome here?" As he posed the question, he reached out, guiding an errant curl from her cheek and tucking it beneath the mobcap she still wore. "Not another of these wretched things. Why do you hide your glory?"

"For ease and propriety," she told him simply. An easy answer. But also, being noticed was not the role of the governess. "And you must know you are welcome, although I ought to be made of sterner stuff."

"I'll admit to being glad you aren't." His grin was in full force now, those maddening dimples appearing. "But may I?"

He gestured to her cap, which was so much a part of Miss Persephone Wren that she often forgot to remove it.

"If you must."

He had scarcely waited for her response before he plucked the cap from her head. With a teasing air that was at odds with the evidence he had recently given his enemies a *drubbing*, as he had called it, he made as if to toss it into the fire he had just stoked. With a squeal of horror, she leapt toward the cap, trying to snag it from his fingers and save it from peril.

But he held it out of reach, and instead, the action merely brought her firmly against his chest. His free arm banded around her waist, anchoring her to him. The rise of him, firm and pronounced, made her hotter still. The ache that had never seemed to completely subside since the night she had spent in his bed blossomed into a throb.

Her hands came to rest on his shoulders, absorbing his easy strength. "You still owe me a mobcap from the last one you burned."

His grin fading, he tossed the most recently confiscated cap over his shoulder instead of consigning it to the flames. "I've a confession to make. I didn't burn your other cap."

"You didn't?"

He shook his head slowly, laying the backs of his fingers against her cheek and stroking gently. "No. I kept it. I rather fancy having a part of you for my own, even if it is that hideous little cap you use to hide your beautiful hair from the world."

She swallowed against a rush of emotion. What could she say? That she had done the same thing with his cravat? Such an admission would cost her too much. She was lying to this man, and she must not forget it.

"You ought to give it back," she said without any sting.

In truth, she adored the notion of this strong, dangerous man keeping her mobcap simply because it was hers.

"But if I can't have you, then the ugly cap is second best." His hand slid around her neck to her nape.

She leaned her head into his touch. "Perhaps you could have me for a time."

"The trouble is, *a time* ain't long enough, lovely." He regarded her solemnly.

What was he trying to tell her? And why did his words make her heart hurt as if barbs had been sunk into that tender organ?

"Stolen moments are all we can have," she told him as much as she warned herself.

It would not do to allow herself to grow any more

attached to him. The bonds which had been forged would
necessarily have to sever. The battle she would need to wage
against Cousin Bartholomew when she reached her birthday
would require all her efforts, persistence, and determination.
But more than that, she heartily doubted a man like Rafe
Sutton would forgive her for lying to him.

How can a lie of omission truly harm him?

She silenced the voice within, for it wanted too much.
The last few years had taught her all too well that she could
never have more, that she was fortunate indeed to have
carved out her little place in the world where she could bide
her time until she reached five-and-twenty.

"I'm greedy where you're concerned," Rafe told her, his
gaze traveling over her face as if it were a wonder to him.

No one had ever looked at her thus, and it chipped away
at her resolve as surely as a chisel. "You never answered me,
Rafe. Why have you come to my room?"

He leaned his forehead to hers. "Because I cannot stay
away from you. Regardless of how many times I tell myself I
ain't the sort of chap for a lady like you, as soon as I'm
beneath this bleeding roof, I'm drawn to wherever you are."

The wall of her defenses had been reduced to rubble. Her
desire rose, stronger than her fear of being caught, more
consuming than the need to maintain her lies and her position as the governess to Anne and Elizabeth. Here, in this
room, she was his and he was hers.

She might pretend for a little while longer that what they
shared never needed to have an end. That forever was possible. That she loved him and he loved her.

"Rafe," she said, but then the profundity of her emotions
overwhelmed her, stealing her capacity for further speech.

Instead, she rose that scant two inches, all she required to
be the same height as him, and pressed her mouth to his. It
seemed she was always the first to kiss, and she was not

certain whether it was by design. Perhaps he was giving her the control in much the same way he had when he had pleasured her. Or mayhap her want was the strongest, the most demanding.

She did not care if it was.

All she did care about was that he was kissing her in return. On a low growl, he cupped her face and held her still while he ravished her mouth with the hungriest kiss yet. He kissed her as if they had been separated for a decade rather than three days. Lips angling over hers, tongue sliding hot and wet to plunder. She made a low sound of her own, desire snaking through her as she sank her fingernails into his shoulders and held on tightly.

Letting him go was no longer a choice. He was a necessity to her. His presence, his warmth, his strength, his kiss. Had she thought the last time would be enough? That she would be satisfied with one night in his arms?

One would never be enough, for she felt every bit as greedy as he had claimed to be. She wanted more. Everything he had to give.

He kissed her harder, exploring, it seemed, every part of her as his tongue swept over hers, tracing her teeth, sinking deep, stroking even the insides of her cheeks. His fingers were in her hair now, the telltale sound of hair pins raining to the carpets, her curls coming unbound to fall down her back.

She did not care.

As if he had helped her dress that morning, he knew where to find all her tapes and ties and buttons. His hands caressed everywhere they traveled, divesting her of each layer with measured motions that were somehow smooth and frantic all at once. Her sensible gown fell away, and with it, all the reasons why she should not be alone with Rafe Sutton in her room. So, too, the reasons why she must not risk everything she had spent all the years of hiding working toward.

She wanted him. He was here. Nothing else mattered tonight. The misery of the last three days without him was forgotten as well. But it was hardly fair that he retained his garments while she was so quickly losing hers. Her fingers moved of their own volition, sliding buttons from their moorings. Untying knots. His coat and cravat were gone before their lips ever even parted.

He was first to break the kiss, lifting his head, his breaths gratifyingly ragged. "I told myself I wouldn't do this. All I wanted was to see you."

She understood he was at war with himself, for it was no different for her. "Seeing is not enough, is it?"

"Damn it." He closed his eyes, his hands tense on her waist, neither pushing her away nor holding her close as he struggled, before opening them on a sigh. "It has to be enough. Christ, what a beast I am. I've already stripped away your bleeding gown."

She wanted him to strip away the rest. Now that he was here, how could she let him go?

"Stay with me," she said, softly, beseeching him with her eyes. "Please, Rafe. I…I missed you."

It was the closest she dared allow herself to get to a declaration.

And it was everything he needed. In the next breath, his mouth was on hers, fiery and insistent. More garments were shed. Petticoats and stays disappeared. His waistcoat and shirt had been shucked as well.

Still kissing, they moved to her small bed. He lifted his head, gazing down at her with so much fiery passion, her knees went weak.

"What is it that you want, lovely?" he rasped, his voice low and rough with desire. "Tell me. I need to know, to hear the words from your sweet lips."

Persephone did not hesitate. "You, Rafe. You are what I want."

"But you're an innocent," he protested, his countenance torn. "You can't mean—"

"I can," she interrupted, rising on her toes to press a swift kiss to his lips, silencing his objections. "I do. I know what I want, and it's you."

Even if this truly was the last time they could be together thus, she wanted to know what it felt like to be loved by him completely.

"Ah, God, you tempt me, woman."

"Take me," she said. "I am yours."

"Mine." His voice was low and deep, an answering spark lighting in his hazel eyes as he said the word.

"Yours."

If only for tonight.

Hands once more firmly on her waist, he guided her bottom to the edge of the bed, then urged her to sit. As he sank to his knees before her, his hands went beneath the hem of her shift, gliding up her calves. Fire followed in his wake, past her knees, where he lingered for a moment, before moving to her garters. These he untied and removed with unhurried motions before rolling down her stockings and removing them.

She sat with her hands folded in her lap, thinking how astounding it was to be here with him, so free. He was bare-chested as she had only seen him once before, and on that occasion, she had been too tangled up in knots over having poured too much of the laudanum in his brandy and fretting over what would happen when he woke in the morning. She took a moment to admire him, all muscle and sinew, the light dusting of golden hair on his chest, the broadness of his shoulders, the protrusion of his clavicle.

"Damnation, lovely, even your bleeding dew beaters are perfection."

"Dew beaters?" She watched in rapt fascination as he laid her stockings and garters on a neat pile before returning his attention to her limbs.

"Your feet," he explained. From beneath lowered lashes, he glanced up at her, flashing the devil's own grin. And his dimples! Lord in heaven, those dimples had appeared once more. "Yours are as beautiful as the rest of you. I should've known."

She felt strangely shy beneath his avid regard. Persephone had never taken particular note of her feet before. "You need not seduce me with flowery compliments now. I know I am not a beauty."

"Ah, but there you are wrong, sweeting." He caught her right foot in both his hands, gently kneading and massaging her sole. "There are few things lower than a liar, and I ain't one of those. If Rafe Sutton calls you beautiful, you're beautiful."

Few things lower than a liar...

She did not want to hear those words. Nor did she wish to think about the lies she had been telling. She had deceived everyone she knew for the last seven years. Strangely, her duplicities had never bothered her before in the way they did now. Lying had been a necessity. It still was. However, for the first time, she truly cared about the family with which she had been placed.

Especially this man.

I love him.

Astonishing thought, creeping into her mind. She'd had it before, but it was as if this moment, this connection with him, granted credence to the emotion in a new way. Rendering it permanent. Real. Undeniable.

She wanted to throw herself at him, kiss him everywhere, show him with her actions how she felt within. And yet, all the rules her joyless governesses had foisted upon her kept her from doing so.

"I am not beautiful, though I thank you for saying so," she said at last, tamping down the ferocious rush of feelings, so new, so queer, so necessary, rising up like the burst of a tiny seedling shooting through the soil in spring.

"You are." He brought her foot to his mouth, bestowing a kiss upon her instep.

"My hair is a dreadful shade of orange," she argued breathlessly as his lips found a sensitive patch of skin on her ankle she had never previously known existed.

Cousin Bartholomew had commented upon the *unfortunate coloration*, as he had called it, which she had received from her mother, whom she had never met. *A true Calcot would never be so distressingly bold*, he had commented once. *Perhaps your mother made a cuckold of your father. I suppose we shall never know for certain.*

Ruthlessly, she tamped down all thoughts of him. Banished his words. In a perfect world, there would be no Cousin Bartholomew, no impediments, no worries or fears or lies. But the world was far from perfect, as was she.

"Your hair is the color of the sunset at its most glorious," Rafe told her solemnly.

He kissed a trail over her shin bone.

She shivered, but not from cold. "I have spots on my nose."

"Copper flecks that mesmerize me." He kissed her inner knees, first one, and then the other.

Oh, his words. They sank directly into her heart, weighing it down like stones.

She struggled to sort her thoughts, find more faults. Heaven knew, her looking glass had always held many. "I am far too tall for a lady."

"You are the perfect height for me." Rafe dragged the hem of her shift higher, until the linen pooled in her lap.

The raiment was thin and smooth from many launderings. A governess could not afford the number of garments a lady could. Not by far. And that was what she was now. A governess. Nothing more, nothing less.

His hands were on her outer thighs, stroking and inciting a new world of sensations. Had she been listing her complaints about her appearance? She quite forgot to recall any others when his hot, hazel gaze met hers.

"I want my mouth on you," he said, his voice rough with desire. "Do you want that, love?"

She licked her lips. "Yes."

Oh yes. Please.

For the last three nights, she had been alone in her bed, dreaming of how it had felt to have his mouth on her. Wondering if she would ever see him again. And now, he was here. On his knees before her, not taking as every man she had ever known had tried to do.

But asking.

Requiring her permission.

She could have wept at the realization, but the roiling emotion inside her gave way to pleasure when he guided her legs apart and his head dipped. His mouth unerringly found her center, sucking on the sensitive part of her. Her pearl, he had said. Finally, a name for the place where her pleasure seemed to dwell, brought to life by him.

Her own fingers had proven poor replacements indeed in his absence.

He sucked hard. She gave herself up to the sensations, wild and streaking through her, furious as bolts of lightning in the midst of a storm. Her hips pumped. He groaned into her flesh, the vibration sending more sparks of desire careening through her, catching flame.

His big, callused hands were not finished with her. He ran them up and down her outer thighs, before catching the hollows of her knees and hooking them over his shoulders.

The position was new.

Decadent.

It forced her to balance herself on her flattened palms on the bed, her legs draped over his back, her lower body tilted toward him as he feasted. And there was no other word to describe what Rafe was doing as he sucked and licked her. The wet sounds of her own excitement echoed in the quiet of the room, joining her pants and his groans of enjoyment. He tortured her so deliciously, swiping his tongue up and down her seam in long, lingering licks before lashing her pearl with swift, fast movements of his tongue, followed by hard sucks. The combination forced her to the edge quickly.

"Rafe," she crooned, mindless, lost to everything but the passion and the pleasure. "Oh, yes." More sounds followed, strange and uncontrollable. Sounds she had never made as the pleasure rendered her mindless.

His rough hands cupped her bottom and tipped her toward him. He rubbed his face against her, the golden whiskers she had so often admired on his strong jaw lightly abrading her sensitive skin.

So sinful.

So wonderful.

He laved her pearl and then paused long enough to lavish praise upon her. "Such a perfect cunny. So pretty and wet. All for me."

"Always for you," she said, feeling wetness slide from her body, trail lower. "Only for you."

"How does this feel?" he asked just before pressing a kiss to her throbbing bud.

"Wondrous," she hissed as his wicked tongue licked up and down her lips, then slid lower, parting her folds, finding the place where her wetness had gathered. He licked into her there, his tongue darting gently at first and then with greater persistence. His fingers gripped her, biting into her rump with painful pleasure. Just when she thought she could bear no more, he sucked hard on her pearl.

Her explosion was instant.

Crying out, she arched shamelessly into him as her inner walls contracted and spasm after spasm gripped her. As the intensity of her pleasure began to slowly subside, her pounding heart returning to a more subdued pace, she became aware of his gaze on her, intense and hot.

His sensual lips were glistening. "God, I love the way you come on my tongue."

She should have been shocked, she supposed, but his sinful confession only made her want him more. "Take me, Rafe. I am yours."

With a guttural sound of pure need, he slid her legs from his shoulders and rose to his feet. "You are sure? If we go too far, there will be no undoing what we've done."

In answer, she caught the hem of her shift and, with a slight lift of her bottom, pulled it off, over her head. She held his stare as she tossed the fine linen to the floor. "I'm sure."

He did not hesitate this time, his fingers flying to the fall of his trousers and undoing them. They slid from his hips, leaving him in nothing but his stockings and his smalls. And then those final barriers were shed as well.

It was not the first occasion she'd had to see Rafe Sutton naked. However, it was certainly the most breathtaking. He was all solid masculine strength, lean and tall, his manhood rising stiff and thick and hard.

And large.

Good heavens! The mechanics of the act which would follow seemed wildly impossible, given his size.

"Don't fret, lovely. I'll go slowly."

She looked up to find him smiling at her with such raw affection that she forgot her trepidation.

I love this man.

How strange and new it all still felt, the realization, the emotions, and the reality of him here with her, nude. About to make love to her.

"I trust you," she said, unwavering.

She knew instinctively that whatever happened between them, Rafe would be gentle and sweet.

He joined her on the bed, taking her lips with his, and she tasted herself in his kiss. They moved together, resting on their sides, bodies flush from hip to chest. His mouth moved lingeringly over hers, lightly at first, and then with mounting hunger. In their passion, they were equals, her tongue the first to delve into his mouth, dueling with his.

His fingers slipped into her hair while his other hand caressed her waist. Between them, his length prodded her belly. She was so caught up in the feeling of his warm skin burning into hers, the languorous seduction of his kisses, that it took her a moment to realize the panic which had previously assailed her at the press of his body against hers was...

Absent.

She was not fearful. The darkness and the memories were still at bay. And all she could think, feel, know, was Rafe, his lips gently moving over hers, his fingers sifting through her hair. His leg moving between hers, insinuating itself. The light friction pleased her, and she arched as he brought his thigh higher until she was riding it.

His hand slid from her waist over her feverish skin. He

cupped her breast, his thumb swirling over the stiff peak as his lips broke from hers. Rafe trailed kisses down her throat, along her bare shoulder, then lower. Over the curve of her breast until he caught her nipple in his hot mouth and sucked.

A cry escaped her.

"Hush, darling girl." He flicked his tongue over her nipple, then painted a lazy swirl around it. "Not too loud."

You are foolish, Persephone.

Making so much noise when anyone in the corridor could hear what she was about. And then where would she be? Utterly, thoroughly ruined.

But oh, what a way to achieve her fall from grace.

"Forgive me," she murmured in a hushed tone. "I was not...*oh*."

He had nipped her, taking her stiff nipple in his teeth and tugging. Her nails sank into the satiny skin of his back. Holding her gaze, he soothed the nip with his tongue, before closing his lips around the peak once more and sucking hard while his thigh pressed against her already throbbing flesh.

"Your cunny is dripping," he said, kissing the side of her breast. "Do you want me?"

She rocked on his thigh, needing more, fingers threading through his blond curls. The sensations buffeting her were exquisite. The first spend he had given her had rendered her almost painfully sensitive there, the abrasion of the coarse hair stippling his muscled thighs stimulating her in a new way.

"Yes," she said, seeking more, her hips moving with a will of their own, tilting to an angle that allowed her pearl to receive the attention she craved.

As if sensing her desperation, he slid his hand between their bodies, his fingers unerringly finding her swollen flesh. The first stroke of his thumb over her, in conjunction with another suck on her nipple, was too much. The second was incendiary.

"There's a love," he crooned, kissing the place where her breasts pushed together. "Come again for me. I want you to spend so many times, you think you cannot possibly spend again."

"Oh, God," she cried, seizing up as his thumb applied more direct pressure, finding the precise location that made her lose control. His wicked words, combined with his knowing touch, were too much.

She stiffened against him, clutching him frantically, as the bliss rolled through her. He held her tightly to him, understanding her need for closeness, kissing her cheek, her ear, her lips, whispering tender words in her ear. To her shame, she realized tears were on her lashes, rolling down her cheeks, as she returned to lucidity, her inner muscles still rhythmically contracting after the force of her pleasure.

He noticed immediately, wiping them away with the backs of his fingers. "Tears, sweeting? Is something wrong? Have I frightened you?"

"No," she hastened to reassure him, amazed she was capable of forming coherent speech. "Nothing is wrong, Rafe. Everything is right."

Too right. And it was both that awareness and the ferocity of her body's physical reaction to him that had led to the overwhelming swell of emotion. Worse, it would never be this right again. She knew it. Had always known it. Rafe was not meant to be hers and nor was she meant to be his.

But they had tonight, and it was not over yet.

"You are sure?" He was frowning, his gaze searching hers, concern etched on his handsome face.

"Oh yes."

She punctuated her reassurance with a kiss and drew him once more flat against her. The length of him prodded her belly, thick and demanding. Her curiosity had a will of its own, and while their tongues tangled, her fingers sought him, circling around the engorged shaft.

He was hot.

That was her first thought.

And sleek and silken in a way that was surprising. Larger, even, than she had supposed. Long and thick. Once more, she wondered how this would work. She possessed a rudimentary knowledge of the marriage bed thanks to life at Silwood Manor and her father's extensive stable. But this was not a marriage bed, and neither of them were horses.

As she gave him a tentative stroke, Rafe moaned and tore his mouth from hers, hips thrusting, pushing him deeper into her hand. The tip of him was wet, and her thumb found this curiosity, sweeping the slickness in circles the way he had done to her.

"Christ." His voice was low and thick, the muscles of his back tense beneath her other fingers. "You will have me spending in your hand if you don't take care."

"Would that be wrong?" she asked, giving him another stroke, this one less tentative, for his body was telling her more than his words ever could.

A strangled sound fled him, his hips moving again. "Ah, lovely. What am I to do with you?"

He kissed the bridge of her nose in what had become a familiar gesture. Perhaps he truly did adore her freckles as he had claimed. She was feeling bold and restless, so she continued what she was doing, moving up and down his shaft. How different and unique a man's body was.

"Do you like this?" she asked breathlessly, watching his gaze as it seemed to change color, the gray flecks becoming more pronounced.

He nuzzled her ear. "I love it. Need you ask?"

She supposed she did not, but words eluded her just then.

He seemed to grow even larger in her hand. An answering ache began deep inside her, one she knew would not be satisfied unless he made love to her.

She kissed his shoulder, his neck, worked her lips over his Adam's apple, the prickle of his whiskers a delight to her already heightened senses. The scent of his soap, lingering on his skin, mingling with musky man, filled her head with fire. Their bodies were entwined, his hardness pulsing in her palm, and she had never felt more alive. It was as if she had been born for this moment, for this man.

As if she had been preordained to love him.

"Please," she said against his skin, inhaling swiftly that she might trap the scent of him in her memory forever. "Make me yours, Rafe. I need you."

"How are you feeling, sweet?" He nibbled on her earlobe, making her shiver. "I do not want to go too fast for you or to frighten you."

It seemed he could not proceed fast enough to Persephone's frenzied mind. But she did not say that. He was being gentle and sweet, so concerned for her welfare. Her heart swelled.

"I want to replace the memories," she told him. "I want there to only be you. Never what happened before."

She was not certain she would be able to banish thoughts of that terrible night or Lord Gregson from her mind forever. But she would try. And memories of Rafe—well, they would take her through her days.

They had to, for she could not have him forever. Only for now.

"It is easier for me to be atop you, at least the first time," he said. "Will you be comfortable on your back?"

It was the position that had given her such troubles previously. The truth was, she had no way of knowing what her reaction would be. The last time had taken her by surprise. Her body had a memory of its own.

"I will try." She kissed his chest, just above his pounding heart. The *thump thump thump* was a steady reassurance. "I know you will never hurt me."

"Never, lovely. Not if I can 'elp it."

His speech had lost its polish. But she liked it that way. She loved the true Rafe, rough and imperfect, hiding beneath all the handsome charm. How fortunate she was to have found this situation; she had to believe it was fated, that she had been meant to meet him. To love him.

She longed to say those words, to tell him how she felt, and yet all she dared was another fervent kiss to his chest. "Thank you for making me feel safe with you."

He tipped up her chin, bringing her gaze to his. "Because you are, sweet. I'll see to it for as long as I'm about."

For as long as I'm about.

There it was, the implication he would leave. And of course he would, as would she. One day soon, they would part ways. It was as inevitable as their paths crossing had been.

Best make this count, Persephone.

She closed the distance between their lips and kissed him, their mouths fusing and melding with a newer, deeper understanding. Slowly, he rolled them until she was on her back and he was settled between her parted legs. But although he continued to kiss her, he did not pin her with his weight. Instead, he leveraged himself on his forearms, careful to keep from covering her as he had done that first night.

He lifted his head and gazed down at her. "How does this feel?"

It felt like Rafe, vibrant and warm and everything she wanted. She never wanted to let go.

"Good," she said through a throat gone suddenly thick,

instead of giving voice to the thoughts flitting through her mind.

He kissed her throat, rubbing his whiskers on her skin. "And this?"

"Also good."

His tongue flicked over her before he kissed to the place where her neck and shoulder met. Softly, he set his teeth there, then kissed away the sting. "What of this?"

"Quite good."

She could feel his lips stretching into a smile against her bare flesh. "I'm improving then, aye?"

He kissed down the valley of her breasts, before taking a nipple into his mouth.

"Yes," she gasped when he shifted his weight to his left arm and used the other to reach between them, petting her lightly.

The swollen bud hidden within her folds throbbed, wanting more.

"What do you think of this, lovely?" He kissed the curve of her other breast, taking his time as he played with her.

She was about to answer when he took her pearl between his thumb and forefinger and lightly pinched. Her hips bucked, white-hot desire shooting through her and leaving her electrified. All she could manage this time was a moan.

"Quiet, sweet," he reminded her, rubbing some more before releasing her and finding her hand. "We'll do the rest together, love. Are you ready?"

She nodded, more ready than she could say. All she wanted was this man.

"Take my cock," he instructed softly.

Cock.

There was the wicked word. How she liked it.

She wrapped her fingers around his length just as she had before, but when she would have stroked him, he stayed her, grasping himself atop her touch. On a slow exhalation that sent his warm breath cascading over her lips, he showed her how to align him with her entrance.

The tip of him pressed against her, in the place where she felt empty without him.

"Will you fit?" she asked as he probed a bit deeper, her worry getting the best of her.

"Ah, heaven and hell and all the saints," he growled. "If I don't, I shall die from wanting you."

She felt the same way.

Another slight movement, their fingers laced together over his cock. This small invasion exhilarated her. Made her angle her hips toward him. And that was when the burning sensation began as she stretched to accommodate more of him. For a moment, she feared he would tear her in two.

He stilled, glancing up at her, his breathing ragged, countenance strained. "More?"

He was asking her if he should stop or proceed. Either prospect seemed equally agonizing at the moment.

"More," she said.

This time, his hips lurched forward, sinking him deeper. He took her fingers from his shaft and raised them to his lips for a reverent kiss. "My brave darling."

Another thrust, and the burning lessened, though the tingling pain lingered, mingling with the new sensation of being filled and claimed.

She clung tight to him, holding the broad planes of his shoulders. He took her lips in another kiss, his tongue tracing the seam of her mouth. One flex of his hips, and he was fully seated, his hip bones pressing into hers, their bodies completely joined.

The sensation was indescribable. Quite unlike what she had anticipated. Her body was so highly aware of every sensation after the painstaking pleasure he had shown her. He was inside her, his cock hot and hard and demanding.

He gazed down at her, his concentration and strain showing. "Shall I continue, sweet?"

Continue?

This was not all there was to lovemaking? She had supposed that, while the precursors had been vastly different from the equestrian form of courting and copulating, the end result would be the same.

She bit her lip. "Horses seem to go about the process a bit differently."

He chuckled, the sound like velvet, warm and soft falling around her. "I ain't a bleeding horse, lovely. And thank Christ for that."

"Oh," was all she could think of to say.

"Shall I?" he asked, kissing one of her distended nipples.

"Yes, please," she said demurely, sinking her fingers into his beloved ringlets.

He was moving the moment her words of permission took shape, his lower body lifting, his cock gliding through her passage and almost slipping free before he slid inside her once more. Slowly, deliciously. And again. This time, her body easily accepted every inch, her bottom rising from the bed to meet his thrust.

His lips met hers, his fingers moving between their bodies to toy with her aching bud once more. The combination of sensation was overwhelming in the headiest sense, their bodies uniting as he fed her kisses and stimulated her pearl until she spent again, seizing with a cry of wild joy as she quivered and clenched around him. He continued thrusting, his low groans blending with her uncontrollable sounds of pure surrender.

Through the exquisite rush, she was dimly aware of him suddenly withdrawing from her, fist wrapped around his length, and spending into the bedclothes. But the loss of him shook her, and she was not ready for it yet. She drew him into her embrace, not satisfied until his body was perfectly pressed against hers, his weight a comforting presence atop her.

He stiffened. "I shouldn't lie on you this way."

But as he tried to frantically extricate himself, she held on tightly. "No, Rafe. I need you here. Right where you are."

He stilled, looking down at her with an expression of such unfettered caring that her eyes pricked with fresh tears. "Whatever you need, lovely."

What if all I need is you?

But these words, like so many others, she tucked away inside. They were better left unspoken. For what good would they do her? Her lies and the truth would eventually collide.

CHAPTER 11

*P*ersephone woke to an empty bed that still smelled faintly of the man she loved and a body that was aching and sore in new places.

And to a terrible, heart-crushing realization.

She had to leave this post.

It was her only choice. Already, she had grown far too attached to little Anne and Elizabeth. Lady Octavia and Mr. Sutton were kind and just employers, the best she had ever known. Mr. Sutton was a man who seemed genuinely concerned about the welfare of not just his family, but everyone in his household. Lady Octavia dearly loved her daughters and wanted them to receive the best education and care possible. But lingering any longer would only be delaying the inevitable.

Because then there was *Rafe*.

He already owned her heart. He always would, and she knew that now. But they came from disparate worlds, and although she had given him her body the night before, she had never given him the truth.

There are few things lower than a liar, and I ain't one.

How would he feel if he knew Miss Persephone Wren was not just a simple governess who had been chased from her former position by a lecherous lord? Would he look upon her in the same fashion once he realized she was Lady Persephone Calcot, daughter to the last Marquess of Silwood, betrothed to the current Lord Silwood, one of the wealthiest heiresses in all England?

Unlikely.

She turned her face into the pillow where Rafe had lain his head, the divot still there, slightly warm. He had stayed for most of the night, then. Judging by the weak light hovering at the edges of the curtains, the hour was yet early. She had just missed his departure, and how she mourned that loss.

For if she did what was necessary, she would not see him again.

Tears stung her eyes. Never see Rafe Sutton's charming grin, his dimples, his golden curls, or his hazel eyes. Never hear his decadent baritone calling her *lovely* once more.

A sob tore from her throat and she buried her face in the pillow to muffle it.

He is not for you, Persephone. You have known that all this time, but you were selfish and you wanted him for your own.

It was true. She had. But last night had seemed laden with endless possibilities that this grim morning light now mocked. She had not been prepared for the magnitude of her grief. She unleashed it now, giving in to the overwhelming sadness as it flowed from her.

When her tears subsided, she forced herself to rise, going to the small pitcher and bowl she kept by the bed and splashing water on her swollen eyes and heated cheeks. Leaving would not be easy, but it had to be done. Her resolve returned. She was mere weeks from reaching five-and-twenty. After almost seven years of hiding in plain sight, her ordeal would soon be at an end.

But she would have a tremendous fight awaiting her. Heaven knew Cousin Bartholomew would not forfeit either her fortune or his power over it easily. He had already proven himself a very dangerous man. She scarcely knew what he was capable of, but she understood that he would stop at nothing to get what he wanted. And ultimately, what he wanted was Persephone and her inheritance. Not necessarily in that order.

With a shudder, she hastily dressed in her unlaundered undergarments from the day before and pulled a clean gown atop them, a no-nonsense affair she could fasten herself with ease, just like her other few, serviceable gowns. When she had been Cousin Bartholomew's unwilling betrothed, he had made certain she had more dresses, undergarments, and hats than she would have ever been able to wear. She had fled without a single one of them, save for the one on her back the night she had run. He had spared no expense in clothing her as would befit his marchioness. But then, the expenses had all come from funds that were rightfully hers.

And what a bitter realization it had been, discovering the ugly, bitter truth. When Persephone had first learned she had been left a vast fortune by her mother, whose family had been in trade and extraordinarily wealthy for it—much to the shame of the Calcot family—she had been shocked. But the swift understanding that her guardian would be in control of it until she either married with his approval or reached the age of five-and-twenty had been brutally disappointing. More so for the man who was her guardian.

When she had been a child, Cousin Bartholomew had scarcely paid her any notice. He had assigned her joyless governesses with a penchant for cruelty, and he had summoned her for periodic reports on her progress or lack thereof. However, he had not been interested in her in the way he had been interested in the chamber and scullery maids, which she had always understood with a despicable sense of relief. Better them, she had so selfishly thought as a girl of twelve, than me.

But when she reached her sixteenth birthday, his disinterest had faded.

She could still recall the way he had looked at her for one of their periodic meetings to discuss the reports he received from her governess. His gaze had lingered on the new fullness of her bodice, and he had asked her to take down her hair. Uncomfortable yet wishing to please him to avoid punishment, she had done so. And he had run his fingers through the strands, declaring the shade was unpleasant to him, but the texture fine enough. Whilst he had been touching her hair, his hand had passed over her breast.

The touch had been most unwanted, and yet, she had seen the expression of sudden, lewd excitement on his face. And even as young and innocent as she had been, she had understood it had been wrong and that later, although she had done nothing untoward in their meeting, she had felt despicably *soiled*.

"Dear God," she whispered to herself now, hands shaking as she fought tears and packed her meager belongings. For so long, she had kept these memories firmly at bay. She had tamped them down, banished them, had stricken them from her mind.

But now that the time had come where she would inevitably need to face him once more, she was reliving each painful recollection as if it had been yesterday. More sobs shook her as she hid the small amount of coin she had been able to secret and carry with her through all her recent situations. Deep within her portmanteau, wrapped in a new pair of stockings she had never worn.

Everything she remembered was a reminder of why she needed to leave.

She had lied to everyone. To Mr. Sutton and Lady Octavia, to Anne and Elizabeth, to Rafe. None of them knew who she truly was, and she did not dare to tell any of them the truth. To do so would only bring unnecessary danger and worry. They all deserved more than that. So much more.

Leaving them would be her gift.

In all the years she had been running from Cousin Bartholomew, this was the first post where she had put the welfare of the family employing her before her own. In the past, discovery by him had been a risk she had been willing to take. She knew he was powerful, spiteful, vindictive, and violent. That he would not hesitate to exact his swift revenge upon her should their paths ever cross again. But now she also feared what he might try to do to the Suttons.

They were not a noble family by birth. Their wealth had been built upon their own tenacity and hard work. One vindictive marquess who had been slowly and steadily building his influence with the aristocracy could ruin them in a month. Perhaps even a week.

Rats would be the least of the worries of the Suttons.

And all because of her.

No, she could not do that to them. Could not bear to think she would cause any harm to the family she had come to know and admire, and most certainly not to the man she had come to love. The man she had given her heart to some time ago and last night had given her body as well.

"Rafe," she whispered to herself, battling a new onslaught of tears. "Oh, my love."

This is what you must do, Persephone. For the greater good of all. Harden your heart and dry your tears.

Yes, that much was true. She was making the right decision. Leaving was what she had to do, not just for Rafe but for the rest of his family as well. She would never dream of inviting danger into their lives.

Though she hated to flee without word, she knew that if she sought out either her employers or Rafe, they would only seek to detain her. And that, she simply could not allow.

She had to leave quickly, before the entire household was awake and anyone would attempt to question where she was going or why. The longer she remained, the more impossible leaving would become. And she cared for this family far too much to hurt them more than she already must.

Everything was packed when she took one last, resolute look around her room.

Heavens, she had almost forgotten the most important object of all, though it was not truly hers, much like its owner. Borrowed, instead. Persephone rushed to her bed, fingers diving beneath the pillow where she had kept Rafe's cravat tucked, and plucked it from its hiding place.

On another sob, she pressed the crumpled linen to her nose and inhaled deeply.

Each day, it carried less and less of his scent.

She could only hope that her memories of him, unlike this scrap of fabric, would remain strong. And for that matter, that *she* would remain strong as well. Summoning her courage, she tucked the cravat into her already stuffed portmanteau.

The time had come to go.

～

"Say that again, brother. I don't think I heard you properly."

Rafe pinned Jasper with a glare, knowing his brother had bleeding well heard him right the first time. He had sought Jasper out this morning just after breakfast, knowing something needed to be done before the day progressed too far.

He had slipped from Persephone's bed in the hush of the night, the weight of guilt heavy upon his heart. He had been reluctant to leave her, but he had also been unwilling to bring any undue harm to her. Being caught in her room would not have served either of them well. And so he had gone.

But as he had crept back to his chamber, feeling like a bleeding cracksman tiptoeing through the house in search of silver, a realization had occurred to him. He could rectify all the potential harms and wrongs in a swift and easy way.

The parson's mousetrap.

That one institution in which he had never supposed he would find himself ensnared. Indeed, the one institution he had done his utmost to avoid at all costs.

"I want to marry Miss Wren," he repeated firmly.

There, he had said it twice, and lightning had yet to streak down from the sky and strike him dead. The clouds had not opened to unleash an unholy torrent of hail. His tongue did not wither and die at the words.

And his heart...

Why, his heart beat on, smooth and strong and assured he was doing what was right. That the decision he had reached was the only possible one he could make. He had fallen in love with her. He had taken her innocence. And now, he would have her at his side. No more slinking from her bed like a bleeding thief.

She would be his.

"Forgive me." Jasper shook his head, as if he was not certain his ears were in working order. "Did Rafe Sutton just declare he wants to wed?"

His brother was having too much bloody fun with this.

He scowled. They were in Jasper's study, an elegant affair that was vastly different from the office he had kept at The Sinner's Palace, which Hart was reigning over at the moment. He'd had his carved desk moved to this town house, however, much to Hart's everlasting disappointment. Hart was currently making do with an old battered affair that was woefully inadequate by Hart's exacting standards.

"If your ears don't work, I'll be more than happy to box them for you," he offered Jasper.

Jasper chuckled, still grinning like a fool. "Considerate of you, but no."

"I could plant you a facer," he suggested, flexing his fingers. "I need to keep up my practice in case we go another round with the Bradleys, and that ugly *rum phyz* of yours could use some rearranging."

His threat did nothing to subdue his brother, however. "My lovely wife likes my face just fine, and hers is the only opinion that matters."

Jasper was hopelessly in love with Lady Octavia, and for the first time, Rafe was able to take a good, long look inside himself and realize he wanted what Jasper had with his wife. He wanted Persephone at his side, in his bed, loving him, raising their children.

Aye, he did. Girls with red curls and her eyes. Mayhap even a Mayfair house of their own one day, especially if The Sinner's Palace II proved as lucrative as he believed it would.

He swallowed against a rush of emotion, realizing his brother was staring at him, expecting him to speak. "You heard me correctly, Jasper. I want to marry Miss Wren."

"You want to marry my governess."

"Anne and Elizabeth's governess," he corrected, acknowledging he did not care for anyone else to think possessive thoughts about his Persephone.

Yes, that was right.

His.

"Don't correct me, stripling." Jasper glared back at him. "I'm your elder."

Rafe squinted. "I *do* detect some gray at your temples."

"Arsehole," his brother said without heat. "I haven't any gray at all."

"Of course you don't," he said in exaggerated fashion, as if he were agreeing just to assuage Jasper's offended sensibilities.

"Back to business, greenhead. What's this about marrying Miss Wren? Do you know how deuced difficult it is to find a governess worth a damn? If you marry her, I'll have to secure another for my hellions."

"Lady Octavia will," Rafe corrected, unable to keep the stupid grin from his lips at the thought of marrying Persephone.

The more he spoke about it, heard the prospect bandied about aloud, the more real it became.

"Here now." Jasper's eyes narrowed. "Why the rush for a wedding? Have you made yourself too bloody familiar with Miss Wren beneath my roof, you rogue?"

Well, hell.

For the first time in his life, Rafe felt a flush come to his face. Even his ears went hot. What could he say for himself?

He could still taste her on his lips.

"A wedding is called for," he said simply, rather than confessing in any detail what he had done.

Protecting Persephone's honor and reputation was of the utmost importance. Not that he gave a scrope about society or propriety, but it stunned him to realize just how much he did care about everything to do with her.

Love.

Fancy how it changed a man.

How it made him whole when he had never so much as noticed he was missing a bleeding thing before it.

"Damn it, Rafe, you've tupped her, haven't you?" Jasper scowled at him, shaking his head once more, all the playful banter between them dissipating in favor of seriousness. "I might have known by the way you avoided answering me when I asked you what was happening between the two of you. Octavia said you would never dare to defile an innocent governess. Said you were trustworthy. I should have told her I know my brother better, but I..."

"But you dislike arguing with your wife," he finished for him ruefully, passing his hand along his unshaven jaw. "Lady Octavia is an angel, and I'm a sinner through and through. I've nothing to say for myself, other than that I'm determined to make amends."

"By marrying Miss Wren."

"By wedding her, aye. That's the ordinary way of a chap to make an honest woman of his lady love, ain't it?"

"The East End way, perhaps." Jasper raked his fingers through his coal-black hair, sighing heavily. "Why did I decide to leave off drinking jackey?"

In his younger years, Jasper had wenched and drank himself to oblivion. But now that he was happily domesticated, he had changed his ways.

Within reason, of course. There were some parts of the rookeries that never left a man.

"Because you're an old married codger with gray hair," he provided helpfully, attempting to lighten the somewhat grim mood of their conversation.

"You are trying me, brother."

"If I wasn't trying you, I'd be gone to Rothisbones."

"I may send you there yet."

The threat did not concern Rafe in the slightest. "Well? What do you say to me marrying Miss Wren?"

"I'm not her father. I can't give you permission." Jasper frowned. "You'll need to inquire with the lady herself, unless you've already done so?"

"No." Rafe grimaced. "I ought to have done. But..."

He had been too busy shagging her senseless.

No need to say that, however, so instead, he allowed his words to trail away.

"I suspect I understand your meaning," Jasper said, his expression one of solemn long-suffering. "What did I ever do to deserve such a wild family?"

Rafe grinned now. "You were born a Sutton. It's in our blood."

"Yes it is. The apple and the tree and whatnot."

"At least we aren't tosspots like our pa was," Rafe pointed out.

Their father had been a scoundrel, through and through. But he and his siblings had banded together with Jasper as their leader. He had saved them all, and every one of them was here to tell the tale.

Except their brother Loge.

Rafe felt a twinge of sadness, mingling with hope the Sutton who had disappeared was not dead but rather alive somewhere in London. But that was a worry for another time.

"At least we aren't that," Jasper allowed before canting his head, studying Rafe with a thorough stare. "Are you in love with her, Rafe?"

Admitting to his feelings felt damned odd. Before, he'd reserved his love for his family only. But there was room in his heart for one more.

"I am," he said simply.

For the first time since reaching his conclusion, he wondered what would happen if she were to deny him. They had shared passion, but that did not mean she wanted to marry an East End rogue like himself, bind herself to him forever. Hell, what would he do if she told him no?

"Then we will have to go and find Miss Wren so the two of you can have an audience," Jasper said.

"You approve?"

His brother grinned. "You hardly need my approval, Rafe. But if that's what you came looking for this morning, it's yours. Even if you are poaching my governess."

Rafe smiled back at him, relief swelling like a balloon about to take flight. "She's mine, Jasper. She ain't yours."

Just then, the door to Jasper's study opened and his wife, Lady Octavia, bustled over the threshold with his nieces, Anne and Elizabeth, at her side. A lovely woman with hair dark enough to match Jasper's, Lady Octavia was the perfect wife for his brother. She was intelligent and caring, and she loved the twins fiercely. She brought a softer side to Jasper that Rafe had never known existed until her presence in his brother's life.

Rafe found himself thinking he had a similar, good-hearted woman in Persephone. How amazing it was that he should have found her, and here beneath his own brother's roof. Surely their meeting had been preordained. A story to tell their children one day.

Ah, Christ. Listen to yourself, Rafe Sutton! You're dicked in the nob, you are. You're growing weak.

He could not argue with the voice in his mind. He *had* grown weak. But he was in love, and he could not be sorry for it. His life with Persephone would be far more complete than his life without her ever could be. He knew that the same way he knew his face in the looking glass. It was familiar, accepted, understood.

"Uncle Rafe," Lady Octavia declared, sending him a strained smile as she clearly attempted cheer for the benefit of the twins. "We have been looking for you."

His instincts told him something was amiss.

He rose to his feet, tension coiling within him.

"Oh? And why is that?" he asked.

Likely, his instincts were all wrong. When was the last

time he had stayed up nearly all night just to gaze at the woman in his bed?

Never.

But he had last night, watching Persephone sleep until at last he had forced himself to leave her room, lest he had fallen asleep there and been seen slipping from the chamber by the early morning hours.

"We supposed we would find Miss Wren with you," Lady Octavia said to him. "Have you seen her this morning?"

Of course he had seen her, sleeping and sated with the glow of the moon in her sunset hair and one rosy nipple peeping from beneath the counterpane.

Do not say that aloud, you bleeding noddy.

He cleared his throat. "No, I have not seen Miss Wren this morning. Why do you ask?"

"She was to begin the girls' lessons half an hour ago, but she is nowhere to be found."

Something shifted in Rafe's gut, twisting. Needling him. Persephone's absence was troubling and quite unlike her, but then, he had taken her innocence the night before. Perhaps she had overslept.

"Have you checked in her chamber?" he asked, trying to combat the rising sense of worry gnawing at him.

"One of the maids did," his sister-in-law said, frowning. "She said it was empty, the bed made and not a trace of Miss Wren to be seen."

Those words made his heart freeze in his chest.

Not a trace of Miss Wren to be seen.

"I want Miss Wren," Elizabeth said with a pout.

Or was it Anne?

Rafe could not be certain. The twins were dressed in identical gowns this morning, and his mind felt as if it had been inhabited by an impenetrable fog.

"She was going to finish telling us about Daisy the Duck,"

the other twin announced. "I want to know if the boat she made leaked, or if it carried her across the lake to the opposite shore."

"Why the devil would a duck need a boat?" Jasper asked, sounding perplexed.

"You mustn't use oaths, Papa," the girls chastised him in unison.

"The duck was afraid to swim," said the twin on the right, who he was reasonably certain was Anne.

"Miss Wren made the story up herself," added Elizabeth.

Or at least, he thought it was Elizabeth.

"If she ain't here, we'll never know the ending!" Anne's lower lip trembled, her hazel Sutton eyes welling with tears.

Christ, he hated the sight of a weeping female. He plucked a handkerchief from his waistcoat and offered it to his niece, bending down until he was on her level. "Here now, dry your tears, lass. What makes you think Miss Wren isn't here?"

She had to be here somewhere. She'd said nothing of leaving the night before. And he refused to believe she would simply disappear on him.

She wouldn't.

Would she?

"Anne said she dreamt Miss Wren came to the nursery to say farewell," Elizabeth added. "And that she would miss us so. Maybe it weren't a dream."

"Maybe it *was not* a dream, dearest," Lady Octavia corrected gently.

Realization thundered into him.

Fucking hell.

His feet were moving, his legs striding, taking him from Jasper's study. Ignoring the confused calls that followed him, he took the stairs three at a time, practically leaping up them in his driving need to get to Persephone's chamber.

She cannot be gone.

She cannot be gone.

She cannot be gone.

With each frantic step he took, the words repeated themselves in his mind, a litany the rational part of him was beginning to suspect was a lie. He was dimly aware of one of Jasper's dogs chasing at his heels in nervous excitement. It was Motley, the young pup, panting and dogging his every footfall.

By the time Rafe reached Persephone's room, desperation led him to throw open the door and race inside, not giving a damn about propriety or privacy. Motley followed him with a loud bark and then an accompanying whine.

The chamber was empty.

The maid had been right.

Not a hint of Persephone remained. The bed he had made love to her in the night before was sternly made, nary a wrinkle on the coverlet. The bedside table was empty. The small wardrobe was barren when he threw open the doors. Nothing remained, save the slightest hint of Winter's soap.

Persephone was gone.

A howl emerged from him, scarcely human, bubbling up. She had left him. Fled in the night at some point after he had gone. Had it been because of what had happened between them? Had she believed he would not offer for her after he had taken her maidenhead?

"Damn it," he muttered.

Motley shadowed him as he paced around the small room, nearly tripping him. With a growl of pure rage and frustration, Rafe swiped at a chair, toppling it over. The action did nothing to diminish the rising anger he felt for himself.

He should have asked her to marry him last bleeding night. If he had, maybe she would have stayed. Motley whined again, then made a low sound of complaint and lay on the floor, resting his head on his paws. Utterly defeated, Rafe sank to his knees beside the dog.

She had disappeared.

As if she might have never been, aside from the ache in his heart to show she had found her way there.

One way or another, he was going to find her. This was all his buffle-headed fault.

Motley licked his coat sleeve and then began chewing on it. Rafe didn't even have the heart to stop him.

CHAPTER 12

*L*eaving the Sutton town house without notice had proven easier than Persephone had anticipated. She had even chanced a hasty visit to the girls' nursery to whisper a farewell one last time.

By noon of the following day, she was ensconced in a small room she had paid far too dear a price for, considering its slovenly state. But never mind that; it was to be expected. Her years navigating London as an unwed lady left her feeling fortunate indeed to have found a room that was at least suitable to live in.

And though her heart was aching and broken, she had resorted to finding her next situation, just as she had half a dozen times before. She had already answered three requests for a governess. However, given her urgent need of a new placement and the current available posts, her choices were lackluster at best and dreadful at worst.

She had been here before. Had done this before. Starting over was no different today than it had been the last time she had done so. She looked at her portmanteau resting beside the tiny bed and tried in vain to conquer a fresh rush of tears.

Rafe's cravat was still tucked neatly within it, placed there with loving care the last time she had extracted it to bring it to her nose for the faintest hint of him.

You did the right thing, Persephone.

Why did doing the right thing feel so terribly wrong, as if it would break her heart in two?

A knock at the door interrupted her thoughts. For a wild moment, her heart leapt as she imagined it was Rafe, coming to collect her. But no, how foolish. He would have no notion of where she had gone. More than likely, it was Mrs. Bridges, from whom she had rented her room.

She went to the door and opened it without thought. And just like that, her world changed.

Her entire body went cold at the familiar form towering over her. Not many men were taller than she. But one man in particular had always been a full head taller, in true Calcot fashion.

"My dear Persephone," Cousin Bartholomew drawled pleasantly, as if she would welcome the sight of him, as if he had been invited or expected. "It feels as if it has been an age since I have last beheld you."

She moved to slam the door on him, but he was too quick, his booted foot keeping her from closing it. "What are you doing here?"

Throwing all her weight against the door, she tried desperately to keep it closed so he could not enter. Her heart was pounding, her mouth dry, desperation seizing her in a relentless grip. Surely this was a dream from which she would soon wake, realizing it had all been a terrible illusion.

"Coming to collect my bride," he answered, using his superior strength to push the door inward.

She attempted to hold fast to the battered plank floors but her slippers were sliding. "If you do not go, I'll scream and Mrs. Bridges will come to see what is amiss."

"Mrs. Bridges is a woman of practicality and good breeding." He wedged his shoulder into the doorway, gaining on her. "She knows I am a peer of the realm and that you are my mad, runaway ward. She will not save you, my dear."

"I am not mad!" she cried out, still pushing with all her might, though it was fast becoming apparent doing so was a losing battle.

"Your denial will not aid your cause," he gritted, giving one more, sudden shove.

Persephone was caught off-balance, and she toppled backward, landing hard on her rump as Cousin Bartholomew gained entrance, closing the door at his back. His countenance was smug.

Victorious.

Hateful.

Her stomach clenched with terror. For so long, she had avoided him. And now, her greatest fear had come to fruition. He had returned, and he intended to take her with him. Just when freedom had finally been within her reach.

She scrambled to her feet, eying him warily.

She did not know if he would pounce or if he would, as he had so often enjoyed doing in the past, toy with her until striking at the moment she least expected it.

"Did you not think I would come for you, my dear?" He tilted his head, considering her, an ugly smile slowly spreading over his thin lips. "Ah, I can see from your countenance you did not believe I would. But then, all these years, and your birthday so near. You must have believed yourself incapable of being found."

Not incapable, but she had begun to feel complacent in a way she had not been in the earlier years of her flight. She could admit as much to herself now. When she had first left Silwood Manor, she had guarded everything with the greatest of care—her identity, her person, her friendship.

The Persephone of seven years before never would have allowed herself to so much as hold a conversation with a man like Rafe Sutton.

But she would not give Cousin Bartholomew the gratification of her acknowledgment. Instead, she kept her head held high and maintained her silence.

He laughed then, as if he found this moment, her at his mercy after fighting him for so long, amusing. But, knowing Cousin Bartholomew, he likely did.

"Ah, my sweet, innocent Persephone, clinging to your hopes like the stupid little romantic you are." He laughed again, but there was no accompanying light of mirth in his light-blue eyes. They were dead, just as they had always been. "I would have thought I had disabused you of your mother's nature when you were a child. But then, the most difficult of spirits to crush is the foolish, hopeful one. Fortunately for me, destroying them also proves the most enjoyable."

She suppressed a shudder, refusing to show him fear, for she recalled all too well how he thrived upon the terror of others and the power he wielded over them.

He reached out with a gloved hand then, the butter-soft leather lightly connecting with her chin, tilting it upward. "You do not imagine I will be gentle with you after the merry chase you have led me on, dearest."

How she hated his use of the endearment. On his lips, it was a weapon. A venomous snake, waiting to strike. Still, she said nothing, refusing to give him her words.

"You must, else you would not be showing such disobedience." His nostrils flared. "Oh, my dear. I can assure you that you will not be treated as you once would have been. I tried to tell you, but you would not listen, how marriage to me would be a wondrous state. All you had to do was please me, and I would have been quite lenient. But a man does not want a soiled bride."

She would have flinched at the condemnation in his voice, but she was doing her utmost to remain calm and unaffected.

"After what you have done with Gregson?" He shook his head slowly, and in an instant, his face changed, the lines of complacency growing harsh and violent, his eyes darkening. He caught her chin in a violent grip so painful she could not suppress her squeak of surprise. "My innocent virgin bride has returned to me a whore. I will be treating her as one."

"I am not your bride," she bit out.

He squeezed her jaw hard enough that she had no doubt there would be bruising there on the morrow. "Yes you are."

"No," she managed to choke out past the pain and the fear. "I am not. You cannot force me to marry you."

His lip curled. "I will not have to force you, my dear. When you consider the choices before you, you will beg to be my wife."

Finally, her rage and hatred for him overcame all else. A rebellious surge rushed through her. She was not the girl he had cowed. She was nearly five-and-twenty. She had lived on her own, in secret, for almost seven years. She had earned her living and worked desperately hard just to be free of him. She would not surrender to this madman now!

Persephone spit in his face.

His reaction was almost instant. He slapped her so viciously, her teeth clacked together, and she bit her tongue. The metallic taste of blood filled her mouth, and her eyes welled with tears, but she refused to blink and allow a single one of them to fall.

Calmly, as if he had all the time in the world, Cousin Bartholomew reached into his waistcoat and extracted an embroidered handkerchief. Like the rest of his clothing, it looked impossibly expensive, and she had no doubt she had paid for it.

Holding her gaze, he wiped the spittle from his lips and cheek. "That was badly done of you, my dear. In time, you will grow to learn that I am a fair man. If you obey me and seek to please me as a proper wife ought, I will be kind to you in return. If, however, you are disobedient, I will be left with no choice but to punish you."

She remembered how much he liked punishment. Just how much it pleased him. Once, as a child, she had unintentionally spied him punishing a chambermaid with a riding crop while she had begged and pleaded with him to stop. Each denial had earned another slap. Sick to her stomach, Persephone had run, too terrified to ask the poor maid what had happened when later their paths had crossed. When she had grown older, she had come to understand there was something unnatural about him. That he *enjoyed* the pain of others.

Much as he was enjoying hers now.

His hand still gloved, he stroked her cheek in a feathery caress, his gaze on the tingling skin he had abused. "How ruddy your skin becomes after it has been struck. Such a pretty flush. I have a suspicion I shall be seeing more of it when you defy me."

He meant to beat her. And he would find pleasure in every moment of it.

"I will not marry you," she said. "You cannot force me into a marriage."

But even as she issued the denial, she knew how weak it was. Cousin Bartholomew was a powerful man with powerful friends, capable of any depravity, willing to commit any sin to further his cause. That was why she had run seven years ago rather than remain at Silwood Manor. It was a miracle she had eluded him for this long.

He'd had control of her fortune from the time her father had died when she had been but nine years old. And he had been determined to do anything and everything in his power to keep her inheritance in his greedy claws.

"If you refuse, I will have your rookeries-born ruffian rat killed."

The dull pulse of dread which had been her constant companion since his arrival in her shabby little room tightened into a cold knot of fear. Surely he could not be speaking of Rafe. There was no way he would know she had formed an attachment with him, that he was the man she loved.

She stiffened. "Mr. Jasper Sutton was my employer, Cousin. He did nothing more than provide me with shelter and fair recompense in return for my labor. He is a fine man and undeserving of your wrath."

"It is not Mr. Jasper Sutton I speak of, my dear." His grin was pure evil, utterly triumphant. "I am referring to his younger brother, Mr. Rafael Sutton. It is he who attacked Lord Gregson."

She bit her inner lip, willing her face to remain an expressionless mask. Refusing to give him any satisfaction or proof he was right.

"Silent, my dear?" Again, one of his cutting laughs. Strange how viciousness could cloak mirth and become so ominous.

If anything were to happen to Rafe because of her, she would never forgive herself.

"Very well," she said. "I will go with you."

Her portmanteau was already packed.

~

"Are you going to spend the rest of your life rattling Saint Hugh's bones and drowning your bloody arse in jackey?" his younger brother Hart asked grimly at Rafe's side.

The interior of The Devil's Spawn was swirling around

the edges of his blurred vision, a state that was likely partially caused by the fact that he could not recall when last he had slept and partly thanks to the gin he'd been drinking all evening.

"Rolling dice is a good fucking distraction," he informed Hart crudely, wondering why he had allowed the arsehole to accompany him this evening.

Hell, had Hart even asked permission? Rafe struggled to sift through the murky shadows of his mind and could not recall how he had come to be here, sitting at the green baize and wagering half his blunt away on what would have once been enemy territory. Their families had been forever joined when Rafe's sister Caro had wed Gavin Winter, putting an end to the feud that had once divided Winters and Suttons.

The devil's arsehole. All he *could* remember was that he had been searching for Persephone for a week, and he had nothing to show for his efforts. Not so much as a damned whisper of her name in all London. And that nothing echoed what was left of his conscience and his soul.

"You're becoming a tosspot like our pa," Hart observed shrewdly.

To that, Rafe raised his glass in mock salute. "I ain't a tosspot. I'm a chap whose heart's been crushed to dust beneath 'is lady's fine beater cases. Have a care now, you bleeding arsehole. I'd 'ate to give you a basting, but I will, lad. Don't doubt it."

Persephone had left him without a word, nary a farewell, and no means of finding her after she had gone. No chance to right the wrongs he had done.

"I'm not a lad." Hart reached out and thieved the glass from Rafe's fingers. "And you've had enough hazard and gin for the evening, brother."

He couldn't have Persephone.

She was lost to him forever.

All he had left was dice and drink.

He attempted to wrest the plunder from his brother's greedy hand, but the bastard was too quick. "Give me my jackey."

"You don't need it, Rafe."

"And since when are you my mother?" he snapped, growing irritated by Hart's attempts at steering him from his course. "I'm older than you by a bleeding year."

Persephone wasn't coming back. After scouring every inch of London, desperation keeping him awake all night long as he tirelessly attempted to find her, he had finally admitted defeat. He'd never see her again. He wanted to lose himself in game and drink. Was that so much to ask for?

Hart clapped him on the back whilst sliding the glass along the table, farther away and out of Rafe's reach. "What do you say we pay a call to The Garden of Flora?"

He could never look at another woman again, for as long as he lived.

"Don't want petticoats," he grumbled. "There's only one woman for me."

"And yet, she's left you," Hart pointed out calmly. "Don't be daft. This bit of skirts wasn't for you. Find a moll and fuck her silly. You'll feel better for it in the morning."

There had been a time in Rafe's life when the notion of hiring one of Sophie's girls for the night and surrendering himself to depravity would have been all he wished. But Persephone was the only woman he wanted. The only woman he would ever want, now and forever. Too blasted bad he had been too stupid to tell her that when he'd had the chance. Maybe she wouldn't have run.

"I don't want a moll." He reached for the gin again and just missed it, but he also managed to upend the glass and send his precious jackey all over the table. "Ballocks."

Something smacked into the back of Rafe's head then. He

blinked, his vision fuzzier than ever. He rubbed his skull, scowling. "What the devil was that?"

"*That* was me." Dominic Winter was hovering over him, a hard expression on his face. "And there's more where that came from if you don't get some sense into that thick pate of yours."

"Winter." Rafe attempted to pin the other man with a glare for having the daring to lay a hand upon him, but his eyes were being deuced difficult thanks to all the spirits he had partaken. Besides that, he was filled with the munificent glow that only a dram—or two, or three—could provide. He was in that transcendent state where he bloody well loved everyone. Or most people. Not Hart. Fuck him, the cursed liquor thief. "*Bene bowse*, old chap. Your jackey is quite good, loath though I am to admit it."

Winter inclined his head. "The patrons of The Devil's Spawn are damned exacting. I aim to please. No baptized spirits here as they will find in other, lesser establishments. But your brother is quite right that you've had enough."

Christ. Not more of this damned fee, faw, fum.

He sighed. "You don't look like my mother, Winter."

"I certainly hope your mother was prettier than I," Winter said, deadly serious. "Given your ugly Friday face, it ain't likely."

He scoffed. "Don't tempt me into giving you the drubbing of your life."

Rafe knew he was by no means in a state to enter into a bout of fisticuffs with Dominic Winter, or any other manner of defending himself, and yet he could not seem to still his tongue. When a man had nothing left to lose, he clung to recklessness, and damn all else to perdition.

Where was his gin? Hart had taken it from him. Why? He needed more. Right bleeding now. Yesterday, in fact. His brother was a heartless arsehole.

Oh, Christ. That was right. He'd spilled it, hadn't he?

"You'll be coming with me, Sutton, or the only one of the two of us receiving a drubbing will be you," Winter said coolly. "Hart?"

Who the devil did Winter think he was? True, this was his family's gaming hell. But this was the goddamned *East End*, and there was neither king nor queen nor prince in these far-flung, dangerous, forgotten streets. There was only keen wits, struggling chaps, and families doing their utmost to make certain they could stay together with a solid roof over their heads, filled bellies, and that ever-elusive feeling of home.

It had taken Rafe all his life to realize his home was The Sinner's Palace. And then, not long after finally welcoming his family's gaming hell as a place of comfort and familiarity and hope rather than darkness, he had realized his true home.

Miss Persephone Wren.

"Rafe?" Hart was asking, his hazel Sutton eyes searching.

Had he said something?

"Eh?" he asked, cupping a hand to his ear as if he could not discern the words his brother was speaking. "Louder, brother. I can't hear a goddamn thing you are saying."

"Winter says he may have word of your Miss Wren," his brother said, raising his voice.

Everything within Rafe froze. "Persephone? Miss Wren? Christ, why did you not say so sooner, man?"

"Come with me, Sutton. I'll see to it you get a filled belly, and then I'll tell you everything I know."

CHAPTER 13

*H*er return to Silwood Manor had been a bittersweet homecoming indeed.

Persephone stood before her beloved mare, Echo for the first time in nearly seven years, holding back tears at the differences which had come to pass in the time she had been gone. Echo was no longer the youthful mare she had once been, and though the stable master had taken excellent care of her, judging from her fine form and healthy coat, her age was apparent in her gait.

But she remembered Persephone. Those brown eyes gazed into hers now with an equine sense of understanding that only served to heighten Persephone's own heartache.

"It is a misery, is it not, Echo?" she whispered to her mare. "What has time done to us, my love?"

Rafe's voice was there, an ever-present memory burned into her mind. How handsome and concerned he had been, the morning when he had hurried her back to her room, taking care to make certain they would go unnoticed.

We'd best 'urry, lovely. Time ain't exactly our bosom friend this morning.

His low rasp, the tinge of an East End drawl, his charm and the tender way he had gazed upon her, remained firmly tangled about her heart. They always would.

Time had not been their bosom friend at all, for it had been far, far too short. And now, she had been forced to return to Oxfordshire and face the wedding she had spent the last few years running from. It was either that or risk the life of the man she loved. Rafe was too precious to her. She would gladly sacrifice her future and her happiness if it meant preserving his.

A tear broke free and ran down her cheek, but she dashed it away before the servant attending her could take note. She had been in Oxfordshire for only several weeks, and the banns had been read. Cousin Bartholomew was leaving nothing to chance. In three more days, she would find herself wed to a man she loathed. One sennight before her birthday, when she would turn five-and-twenty.

She supposed that was why he was allowing her this small concession, the permission for a short ride without either a groom or himself as accompaniment. At least, according to the groom. He had said nothing of his intentions over break-fast when he had declared she might enjoy a turn about the stables since she had been an *obedient betrothed* since their return.

Oh, how those words had infuriated her. And how she had longed to throw her half-eaten eggs and kippers in his face. But she had not. Instead, she had calmly thanked him and inquired whether or not he would like to accompany her. He had declined, much to her relief.

In truth, Cousin Bartholomew was an abysmal rider. His large form and uneasiness with horses—brought upon by a childhood accident in which he had been thrown from a saddle—made him an awkward rider, looking always as if he were an inch from spilling to his doom. He had never cared for horses, aside from their monetary value or the éclat they afforded him.

"She is ready, my lady," the groom said, interrupting her tumultuous musings. "His lordship expects your return in one quarter hour. You'll want to be gentle with Echo as she's occasionally been favoring her front leg on cold mornings."

He was new here, like so many of the domestics at Silwood Manor. Cousin Bartholomew had changed much, she had discovered in her return, and she could not help but to wonder who had paid for all his revisions. New servants, the construction of a lake and fountain in the valley Silwood Manor overlooked, a Palladian pavilion on the front façade, fresh carpets, a small fortune in paintings dotting the new wall coverings.

All while she had been living on the meager wages of a governess, forced from one situation to the next, just for the chance to no longer suffer his tyrannical rule.

She nodded politely to the groom. "Thank you, sir. I will be back in a quarter hour, as his lordship wishes, and I shall take great care of Echo."

Considering she is my horse.

Echo, like many of the horses here at Silwood Manor, was a part of her inheritance. Her mother's side of the family had been mad about horseflesh and rich as Croesus. And Cousin Bartholomew stood to benefit greatly from that combination.

With the groom's aid, she mounted Echo. Although years had passed since she had last ridden a horse, being seated upon her mare's saddle felt as familiar as if she had last been there just yesterday. With her thanks to the groom, she departed, taking care to keep Echo's pace slow and even. She was not limping today, but if Persephone saw the slightest hint of arthritis, she had every intention of dismounting and returning to the stables by foot.

For now, the chance for freedom, even only one quarter hour of it, beckoned with a temptation she could not ignore. The wind on her cheeks was slashing and cool. But at least the gray clouds overhead had not lived up to their ominous portent of rain.

Yet.

She decided to take Echo on their old favorite route, down the lane to the path that circled what had become Cousin Bartholomew's lake. It was a rather gargantuan affair, with a swan presiding over its smooth surface, and Persephone despised it as much as she loathed the life she was about to consign herself to here.

Oh, Rafe.

Where was he now? What was he doing? She hated allowing her mind to wander and wonder, but how could she not? In her old life as Miss Wren, she would have been happily ensconced in the sunshine-filled Mayfair nursery with Anne and Elizabeth. On occasion, they had been accompanied by one of Mr. Sutton's dogs. Usually Motley, who possessed a particular affinity for Rafe.

She could not blame the pup, for she felt the same way.

There was something about Mr. Rafe Sutton. She was sniffling again by the time she and Echo had rounded a copse of trees, blotting out the sight of Silwood Manor sitting loftily on the hill. Weeping was an almost constant state for her now, unless she knew she would be facing Cousin Bartholomew. Tears vexed him mightily, and she had learned he was not averse to showing her just how much during their journey to Oxfordshire.

The bruise had faded, but she had not forgotten.

Her tears were reserved for moments of solitude now, like this one.

She was so lost in her misery that she failed to hear another rider approaching until he was almost upon her. For a wild moment, she feared it was Cousin Bartholomew come to denounce her for her willful disobedience, until she took note of the man's form. He was not as large as Cousin Bartholomew.

And he had blond curls beneath the brim of his hat.

Her heart leapt. Surely it could not be Rafe! Here? In Oxfordshire? No.

She was dreaming.

"Persephone!"

His voice reached her, familiar and deep and laden with an emotion she could not define.

It was him. Somehow, Rafe Sutton was racing toward her on the back of an Arabian gray. She blinked furiously, sure she was somehow ascribing his traits to someone else. For how could he be here, at Silwood Manor? And how would he have known where to find her?

As the questions swirled, her body overtook her mind, and suddenly, she was riding toward him, heart leaping. Each gallop of Echo's hooves brought her nearer, Rafe's giving more credence to the wild and unbelievable notion that he had somehow come to her.

"Rafe!" she cried, pushing Echo as fast as she dared, unable to shake the fear he would disappear before she could reach him.

Their mounts pulled abreast of each other and they reined in at once. Persephone slid from the saddle at the same time Rafe dismounted, and in two steps, she was flying into his arms. Their collision was so forceful, her teeth knocked together and she bit her tongue, but she did not care.

All she did care about was Rafe's arms closing around her, strong and protective. His scent, mingling with the fresh earth and grass and the sharp scent of autumn leaves drying and falling to the ground.

"Ah, God, lovely." He pressed his cheek tight to hers, his hot breath falling on her ear. "I've missed you."

She clung to his neck, tears streaming down her cheeks. "How are you here?"

"I rode the bleeding horse behind me."

His unexpected attempt at humor caused her laughter to burst forth, mingling with the sobs. "I saw you on the horse. What I meant to say was how did you find me? How did you find me here, in Oxfordshire?"

She had never mentioned her past to him, and when she had left the Sutton town house, she had left without divulging her true name or a hint of all the shadows and secrets that kept her running.

"Long story we haven't the time for." He reared back, his hazel gaze traveling over her face as if he had just been presented with a miracle. "Will you ride with me?"

Fear crept over her. "Where? Cousin Bartholomew only allotted me one quarter hour. He will note I have not returned and come riding after me."

"That arsehole didn't allot you any time to ride." Rafe scowled. "Did you think he would allow his prisoner to slip from 'is fingers so easily?"

"How do you know?" She searched his face, his gaze, seeking answers.

"The groom aiding you was one of my men. It's all part of the plan, lovely."

"The plan? You have a plan?" Her heart was beating so fast, relief and love and hope at odds for supremacy. But lingering beneath the surface of it all was fear.

The fear Cousin Bartholomew would find them, that he would do Rafe harm as he had threatened.

Rafe grinned, his dimples appearing. "I would've thought you'd noticed by now, sweet. Rafe Sutton *always* has a plan."

Of course he did, and at the moment, it would seem his

plan involved rescuing her. Which was everything she wanted, except that she could not possibly allow him to endanger himself and his family by incurring Cousin Bartholomew's wrath.

"Cousin Bartholomew threatened you," she blurted. "He told me he would have you killed. I cannot go with you, Rafe. I could never forgive myself if any harm befell you, knowing it was because of your association with me."

"Is that why you left without word? You were trying to protect me?"

"My cousin is a dangerous man," she said, rather than giving him the exceedingly complicated answer to his question. There was not the time for it.

Rafe's dimples disappeared, his countenance turning hard and serious. "I ain't afraid of the Marquess of Silwood."

He knew Cousin Bartholomew's title?

But then, of course he did. He was here, at Silwood Manor, was he not? He had found her.

"You *should* be afraid of him, Rafe. He is a powerful man, a peer of the realm." And heaven knew that a different set of rules applied to lords. A lowborn man like Rafe Sutton would scarcely stand a chance against Cousin Bartholomew's vengeance.

Rafe frowned, his jaw tightening. "Has he given you cause to fear him, sweet?"

Of course he had. Cousin Bartholomew was dangerous.

She wetted her dry lips nervously, the tightness in her chest growing more pronounced. "Please, Rafe. You do not understand the way of it. You must go. Save yourself. I have already agreed to marry him, which has been his plan from the moment my father died and he became my guardian."

"You intend to marry him?" Rafe winced as if he had been struck. "Truly, Persephone?"

Tell him yes. Tell him yes to save him. His pride will make him leave. It is for the best.

Oh, it was too dratted difficult!

Her eyes fluttered closed for a moment as she considered her response. "I..."

"Say the words," Rafe ground out. "Tell me he is the man you want. Tell me you want to marry him. Do that, and I'll go. You'll never see me again."

Never see him again? She had told herself in an endless litany since Cousin Bartholomew had discovered her in London that she would accept her fate. That she and Rafe were not meant to be together, and that if she could not have him, she may as well surrender to marrying Cousin Bartholomew if it would keep Rafe safe. But now Rafe was here, holding her in his arms. How could she possibly tell him that she wanted Cousin Bartholomew, and that she was choosing him over Rafe?

The man she loved was before her. Rafe Sutton, with his blond curls worn too long for fashion, his easy smile and charm, his dimples, ready wit, and the sweet tenderness he seemed to reserve for only those closest to him...the man who had renewed her faith in trust and made her hope again. He was the man for her. He would *always* be the man for her.

"Say it, Persephone."

A gentle mist had begun to fall, and the wind kicked up, making the cold drizzle pelt her in the face as she struggled to form the words.

"You can't, can you?" He cupped her cheek, his gloved hands cool and yet retaining some of his warmth. Enough to chase the sting of the wind. "You can't tell me you want to marry Silwood. Because it would be a lie."

"Everything in my life has been a lie for the past seven years," she blurted. "What would be one more, if it means keeping you safe?"

"Don't do this to yourself, lovely." His hazel eyes were boring into hers. "Don't do this to *us*."

"There is nothing else I can do."

He kissed her then, his mouth crushing. Familiar. Warm. Home.

Hers.

He tore his lips from hers far too soon, forcing her to hold his gaze. "You can come with me now."

Hope rose, fervent and foolish. "But Cousin Bartholomew has threatened you."

"Threats don't scare me, and neither does your arsehole of a cousin."

She believed him. "You do not know what he is capable of in the way I do."

Another gust of wind blew, threatening to tear the hat from her head. Their horses were moving restlessly, reminding Persephone of just how precarious this moment was.

Rafe remained unmoved, his countenance harsh, determination evident in the rigid set of his jaw. "Let him come to the East End for me. I'll be waiting, and it ain't going to end well for 'im."

Of course he would want to protect her, even at his own expense. He had done so before.

She shook her head, the denial cutting through her heart as viscerally as a knife. "No, Rafe."

His beautiful lips tightened. "Why did you leave?"

"Because I had to." *Because I love you, and I lied to you.*

If he was here, he knew she had lied.

Didn't he?

The rain was falling with increased determination now, the mist turning into fully formed drops. In no time, they would be soaked to the skin if it turned into the deluge the distant leaden skies promised.

"Is it because you fear what he'll do to me?"

"No." A shiver tore through her, desperation and sadness chasing the initial elation that had lit her up like fireworks. "It was because I was living a lie, and I could not bear to remain, continuing my charade, knowing I would lose you."

It was the closest she dared come to admitting that she loved him.

He caught a tear on her cheek with his thumb. "Why would you lose me?"

"Because I have been lying to you, and because I feared you would not forgive me when you discovered the secrets I have been keeping." *And because you never told me you loved me, and my heart will always belong to you.*

"You were lying to protect yourself, lovely. I understand. There ain't a bleeding thing to forgive. Come with me now. I'll keep you safe. I vow it on my life."

He was so earnest, and he was looking at her now with such unguarded reverence that a new torrent of tears emerged, mingling with the rain.

"Oh, Rafe. Where would we go? There is nowhere Cousin Bartholomew will not find us now."

"I'm staying at Abingdon Hall as a guest of Mr. Devereaux Winter. We'll be safe there until I can get us to London."

Abingdon Hall was the neighboring estate.

Which meant that flight might truly be possible.

But Rafe had still said nothing of love or marriage.

"Have you come to rescue me?" she asked, needing to know. "What shall we do after we return to London?"

"We will be married, if you wish it. And if you don't, you'll still be better off than you are here, forced into marriage with your scoundrel of a cousin."

Marriage. To Rafe. Her heart leapt at the chance, foolishly rejoicing. She would love nothing better. But if he was offering only because of the terrible circumstances in which she had found herself, out of pity, or because he felt that he had to do so, she would not be able to bear it.

"You do not have to marry me to save me from my cousin or out of some sense of obligation because of what happened between us."

"Is that what you think?" He kissed her again, swiftly, deeply, and she tasted the salt of her own tears and the earthiness of the rains on his tongue. "Did that feel like a bleeding obligation to you? Did it feel like I am only worried about your cousin?"

"No." She bit her lip, studying his beloved face, trying to understand him.

"What it should have felt like is the kiss of a man who loves you, Lady Persephone Calcot," he said, "because that's what I damned well am. I'm the man who loves you."

Her real name.

He had used her full name.

And he loved her.

Rafe loves me.

It was seemingly impossible yet wonderful, like the luminosity of the stars in the night sky.

"You love me?"

"I love you." He was solemn, stroking her cheek, patient and strong.

Wiser than she was. Why had she run from him?

Here is your chance, Persephone. Worry about repercussions later.

"I love you too, Rafe." She turned her head, pressed a kiss to his leather-clad fingers as the rain came down faster and harder. "I shall go with you."

He kissed her again, his lips smiling against hers. "Thank Christ, lovely."

CHAPTER 14

*T*he Marquess of Silwood arrived at Abingdon Hall with more haste than Rafe had anticipated after sending word that Persephone would not be returning to Silwood Manor and that she would instead be remaining at Abingdon Hall. But then, when a man stood to lose as much as Silwood did, desperation often proved an excellent motivator. And Rafe had been hoping for just that.

He was prepared, and not just with the pistol secreted in his waistcoat or the blade hidden in his boot.

"Where is my betrothed?" the marquess demanded coldly.

Silwood was a tall man, broad shouldered, and uglier than the devil. More mean-spirited, too. His massive form, along with the tales Persephone had shared of his appetite for inflicting pain on others, made it more than clear to Rafe why she had feared him. And why she had been so convinced he would truly see Rafe murdered. But Rafe didn't scare easily, and he was more than prepared to take on the Marquess of Silwood.

And he'd win, too.

Rafe flashed the other man a smug smile, clasping his

hands behind his back as if he were utterly at ease. "She ain't your betrothed, Silwood."

The marquess's nostrils flared as if he scented something malodorous. "The banns have been read. Lady Persephone is indeed my betrothed, and I demand to see her. Send for her now."

"You can make demands all you like, my lord, but it won't change a bleeding thing. Lady Persephone ain't going to marry you. She's going to marry me." And as he said those words, his chest felt as if it expanded to fill the entire room.

Persephone loved him. She wanted to marry him. He was happier than any man had a right to be, and he would do everything and anything in his power to make certain the Marquess of Silwood couldn't do a goddamned thing about it.

"That is absurd," Silwood snapped, spittle flying from his lips. "She is the daughter of a marquess. She would never stoop so low as to wed a baseborn criminal from the rookeries such as yourself. If you insist on prolonging this farce, I'll have no choice but to involve the law."

"The law, eh?" Rafe's grin deepened. "I'm sure the law would find a great deal of interest in you and the funds you've thieved from Lady Persephone's trust."

Silwood's face turned a mottled shade of red. "I have not thieved a farthing of my betrothed's trust. How dare you suggest otherwise, you vile cur? Any expenses that have been extracted have been for her benefit."

Rafe was deuced grateful for the Sutton's friendship with the Winter family. If it had not been for Devereaux Winter and Dominic Winter's timely intervention, Persephone would have allowed herself to be forced into marrying this miserable sack of cow shite.

"On the contrary, my lord," he said smoothly, knowing he possessed the advantage in this battle of theirs and understanding the Marquess of Silwood wrongly believed he did. "You have been using Lady Persephone's inheritance to fund your gaming habits. But unfortunately for you, your luck at the green baize is bloody dreadful. You have written more vowels than you will ever have a prayer of repaying unless you get your greedy hands on her entire fortune. Ain't that right, Silwood?"

He could see the moment his words began to puncture the marquess's shield of invulnerability. The quality always believed themselves omnipotent. They'd been born to wealth and privilege, fine educations, the best of everything. Sooner or later, however, men like Silwood discovered they were not as untouchable as they believed themselves.

And what a privilege it was to be the one to bring the Marquess of Silwood low.

The man had kept Persephone beneath his thumb until she had fled, and even then, she had been so desperate to escape him that she had spent years in hiding as a governess who had also been at the mercy of others. The debts he had been incurring at The Devil's Spawn had been enough to catch Dominic Winter's notice, thank God. As had the questions he had been asking, along with rumors he had befriended Viscount Gregson. From there, Rafe had been able to find the rooms Persephone had taken, and he had learned she had left in the company of none other than the Marquess of Silwood.

The truth had unraveled. Gossip had long been swirling about the mysterious disappearance of Lady Persephone Calcot. Jasper's wife, Lady Octavia, had heard the tale many times but had never realized Miss Wren and Lady Persephone were the same until Rafe had torn apart London trying—and failing—to find her. Uncovering the rest of the information he had needed had proved simple. Learning

Abingdon Hall bordered the Marquess of Silwood's lands had been a timely discovery.

"You know nothing," Silwood spat. "Who do you think you are?"

"Rafe bleeding Sutton," he said calmly, holding his ground. "Don't forget it."

Silwood's lip curled. "Do you know what I could do to you?"

Rafe raised a brow, unaffected. "Nothing. That's what you'll be doing to me, Silwood. Do you know why?"

"I did not come here to play games with you, Sutton. I came here to collect Lady Persephone." The marquess took a menacing step forward. "She belongs to me."

"You are wrong."

The voice from the doorway took Rafe by surprise as much as it did Silwood, he was sure. He turned to find Persephone standing at the threshold, an expression of defiance on her lovely face. Damn it, he had told her it would be better for her to remain unseen by the marquess.

Beyond his dastardly reach.

"Dearest," Silwood said coolly. "Whatever is this nonsense? I insist you return to Silwood Manor with me at once."

"No," Persephone said, her voice ringing firmly and loudly as a bell. "I will not be returning to Silwood Manor with you. Because I do not belong to you. I belong to no one but myself."

Although Rafe wished she had listened to him and stayed far away from the marquess, he knew a moment of fierce pride, watching her defend herself. She was strong, his woman. The only reason she had agreed to sacrifice herself to the callous blackleg before him was to save Rafe.

"Have you forgotten what we discussed?" The marquess was moving toward her.

But Rafe was having none of that. His long-legged strides took him to stand between Persephone and her odious cousin. She did not need him to defend her, and Rafe knew it. But by God, he would anyway, until his dying breath.

"Not another step in her direction," he warned Silwood.

The marquess halted, a glower darkening his features. "Are you daring to threaten a peer of the realm, Sutton?"

"Of course not," he said, careful to keep the worry from his voice. There was every chance this plan of his would not proceed as he hoped. But he would fret over that later, in the event he needed to do so. "I am merely advising you, Silwood. Lady Persephone will be reaching five-and-twenty soon."

"Her age is immaterial," Silwood growled.

"It is not," Persephone denied, stepping forward until she stood at Rafe's side, so near, the skirt of her gown brushed his legs. "You know as well as I that turning five-and-twenty means I shall be capable of inheriting the trust left me by my mother."

"Not if you marry first, and without my consent to the marriage," Silwood countered, sounding smug. "You cannot believe I would ever give my permission for you to marry an East End rat such as this. He may be occasionally capable of aping his betters, but he is a lowborn scoundrel. Your father would never have allowed it, and neither shall I."

"That is where you are mistaken, my lord," Rafe interjected smoothly. "You will approve of my marriage to Persephone."

"Never!" the marquess bellowed.

"You seem to be confused about where you stand, my lord marquess," Rafe said, "so I will pay you a favor. You are in debt to The Devil's Spawn for more blunt than you can hope to repay. Lady Persephone is willing to generously settle your debts as long as you accede to her wishes. You have also been stealing from Lady Persephone's trust for years. And then, there is the matter of your maids."

The marquess paled. "What of my maids?"

"Did you think belowstairs doesn't gossip, Silwood?" Rafe shook his head. "Of course you did. Well, you're bloody wrong. They do talk, and quite a bit, especially for the right price. I also happen to know of a scandal journal that's about to print an article about the villainous Marquess of S., who beats and ravishes his maids and has already sired three bastards."

"You are lying."

Rafe smiled. "My mind ain't devious enough to imagine such a vile thing on my own, Silwood. The choice is yours. You can accept my impending marriage with Lady Persephone, or you can suffer the consequences for what you've done."

By one means or another, Rafe had every intention of forcing Lord Silwood to pay for his sins. But first, he needed to be certain he had extricated Persephone from the bastard's clutches without fear of reprisal. He did not need her inheritance by any means. He had plenty of his own coin thanks to The Sinner's Palace. However, the funds were hers by right, and he would be damned if he would allow them to continue supporting a despicable wastrel.

The marquess was clearly at war with himself. His greed made him want to fight to keep Persephone and her wealth in his control. But his sense of self-preservation made him question Rafe's claims about the scandal journal.

"Do not doubt me, Silwood," he advised. "The scandal journal will be more than happy to print every despicable detail, and you'll be ostracized from polite society. And when Lady Persephone pursues the matter of all the coin you've thieved… I don't need to tell you it ain't going to go well for you, Marquess."

"I am marrying Mr. Sutton," Persephone said then, "with or without your permission."

"Defying me is not wise," Silwood cautioned her. "I am a dangerous enemy to have."

Ha! The bastard had convinced Persephone that he would dare to have Rafe killed. But Rafe knew differently. And he had his own protection in the guards at The Sinner's Palace. Even supposing the marquess was able to hire someone to go after Rafe, there were risks he was willing to take in the name of the woman he loved. Keeping her from the clutches of her vile cousin did not require second thought. Nor did making her his wife.

"The only dangerous enemy to have is a Sutton," he told the marquess. "You trifle with me, and you trifle with the whole bleeding family, Silwood. There's a warning from me to you, and that's the last one you'll receive. The next time I have to tell you, it ain't going to be pretty and polite."

"I am not afraid of a lowborn rookeries rat like you." Silwood's lip curled into a sneer.

He gave the marquess his most lethal smile. "You ought to be, arsehole."

Once more, Silwood's nostrils flared. He turned to Persephone, his hands clenched in impotent fists at his sides. "You have a choice to make, my dear. Marry me and hold your head high as the Marchioness of Silwood, or marry this swine and lower yourself to the mud with him."

Persephone raised her chin, regal and beautiful and so very strong. "Mr. Sutton is a better man than you could ever hope to be. I could know no greater honor than becoming his wife."

Pride swelled in Rafe's heart, along with love. "There's your answer, Silwood. If you dare to cause any problems for her, you'll be answering to me and all the rest of the Suttons."

"The Winters as well," said Devereaux Winter as he

crossed the threshold, unsmiling. "I trust I need not tell you how poorly it will go for you if you attempt to cause any trouble for Lady Persephone concerning her trust when she reaches five-and-twenty. My solicitor is prepared to aid her in her cause."

"You will regret this," Silwood vowed, bitterness lacing his voice as his eyes traveled the room, lingering longest on Persephone.

"No." She shook her head, smiling. "I can assure you I will not."

"Get out of my home, Silwood," Winter said curtly, an order rather than a request.

The marquess, having been dismissed and denied what he had been determined was already his, was left silently fuming. And without recourse, too. For a man who thrived on power, this must be a truly low moment. How Rafe wished he could plant the bastard a facer. But he was doing his damnedest to do everything right for Persephone's sake.

"Do not come begging me for another chance when you realize the mistake you have made," the marquess bit out, before offering a mocking bow.

"I shan't," Persephone assured him wryly.

As the marquess took his leave, Persephone's fingers tentatively sought Rafe's at his side. A deep, thrilling sense of possibility came over him. After the weeks spent without her, the relief was enough to make his bleeding knees quake. Not that he would ever admit as much aloud.

"I can't begin to thank you enough," he told Devereaux Winter.

Winter gave him a small smile. "Reserve your gratitude for my lovely wife. She adores nothing so much as aiding a love match."

"Thank you both," Persephone said. "I shall never forget your kindness."

Winter cleared his throat, looking a bit uncomfortable with all the gratitude being directed toward him. But then, Rafe reckoned it was not every day that an East End rogue and a sunset-haired lady had a verbal duel with a despicable marquess in his drawing room.

"We are pleased to help," said Lady Emilia Winter, beaming as she crossed the threshold of the drawing room to stand beside her husband. "We are almost family. Suttons have become treasured friends of the Winters, and, Lady Persephone, my parents held yours in highest regard."

"Still, you would not have had to involve yourselves," Persephone countered, "and risk my cousin's wrath."

Devereaux Winter smiled for the first time, and his expression said everything Rafe needed to know about how the man had come to rule such an impressive empire. "I can assure you, Lady Persephone, it is the wrath of the Suttons and Winters he ought to fear, not the other way around. Lord Silwood's pride has been badly bruised, but he will discover quickly that he cannot bully those who are more powerful than he."

"And if he does not?" Persephone asked, clearly still fretting.

But then, he could not find fault in her fears. She had spent nearly seven years of her life hiding from the man, fearing him and the power he wielded over her. For that power to so suddenly be severed would require time for her to accept. And he would be here for her, in whatever manner she needed.

He gave her fingers a gentle squeeze. "If he does not, then he will find himself in more trouble than he could have imagined."

"I suppose I will not feel truly safe until we are married," she said.

Nor would he. Persephone as his wife was a heaven that

had seemed beyond his reach the last few weeks. "I cannot wait for the day, love."

"Oh, Mr. Winter," Lady Emilia said, pressing a hand to her heart. "Look at the two of them. Do you remember when we were young and in love?"

"As I recall, it has only been three years since we wed," Mr. Winter told his wife with a wry smile.

"Has it?" Lady Emilia was looking at her husband with blatant adoration. "It feels as if you have had my heart forever."

Rafe would have been damned embarrassed—perhaps even a bit disgusted—if he did not feel the same way about the woman at his side. Already, he could not fathom a day when he had not known her. She had always been his, just as he had always been hers. He fully believed they had been meant to be together. Made for each other. And nothing and no one had been able to keep them apart.

He turned to Persephone, heart full. "I well understand the sentiment."

She smiled back, tears shining in her eyes. "So do I. You have my heart, and it will forever remain yours."

"Do you promise?" He was so bloody tempted to kiss her nose and that beloved constellation of copper flecks adorning it.

But they had an audience. Kissing her at all would have to wait, much to his dismay. His lovely was more than worth it, however.

"I promise," she said.

EPILOGUE

"*M*ay I?"

Persephone paused in the act of unpinning her hair and met her husband's gaze in the long, gilt-edged looking glass. "Of course."

Husband. What a thrill that word still gave her, though they had been married for two months now. He settled his hands on her shoulders and pressed an open-mouthed kiss to the side of her neck, then nuzzled her throat. "Mmm. I ought to have thanked Devereaux Winter for his soap in addition to his help with routing your despicable cousin. I adore the way it smells, lingering on your skin after your bath."

The mention of Cousin Bartholomew, who had died suddenly just days following their wedding, no longer brought with it the accompanying dread and fear. He had been killed in a carriage accident. Fate had made certain he would never be a threat to either herself or Rafe, or anyone else, ever again. The new marquess, a distant country cousin, seemed kind and genuine, a happy turn of fortune for all.

Persephone could only hope the servants would be better

treated. She and Rafe had offered all the domestics at Silwood Manor an opportunity to find placement with them in their new household prior to her cousin's death. She had also situated Echo and her other horses quite comfortably now that she had a stable of her own. Echo and the others were happy in the mews at the town house Persephone and Rafe had taken together, not far from The Sinner's Palace II, and quite near to Jasper and Lady Octavia's home. The Suttons had welcomed Persephone with open arms and hearts, and she could not be more grateful to call them family.

At long last, she had found a place where she belonged. A place that was meant for her. A man who was meant for her.

"Mr. Winter may have been scandalized had you mentioned your appreciation for the scent of his soap on my skin before we were wed," Persephone told her husband teasingly, reaching for Rafe's left hand and guiding it to her breast.

She was wearing nothing more than a gossamer night rail which had been designed by London's most sought-after *modiste*, Madame DePlessier, specifically with Rafe in mind. His thumb unerringly found the distended peak of her nipple, his other fingers skillfully caressing. She arched into his knowing touch.

"Winter doesn't seem the sort of cove who scandalizes easily." Rafe's lips grazed the shell of her ear as he spoke, but he kept their bodies carefully separate though they stood together, heightening her eagerness.

She shivered, but not from the cold. "Perhaps not."

He plucked at her nipple, rolling it between thumb and forefinger before giving it a tug. "Don't suppose it matters now. I behaved myself."

She smiled at their reflections. He was wearing a banyan of midnight silk, curls catching the candlelight and giving off a burnished glow. A thin slice of his strong chest was visible beneath the garment. Just enough to tempt. His feet were bare, his masculine calves peeping beneath the hem.

"I rather enjoy when you do not behave, husband," she said, watching as he swiftly dismantled what was left of her coiffure with his other hand.

"And I enjoy the way you look in this gown. It's so bleeding sheer, I can see the pretty pink of your nipples through it."

His low rasp sent heat to pool between her thighs. "You approve, then?"

"Need you ask?" He finished with her hair and spread the wildly curling strands down her back before burying his face in her crown and inhaling. "God, lovely. I can never get enough of you."

"Mmm." She sighed as his right hand joined the left, cupping her breast through the thin fabric of her gown. "I feel the same."

Each day brought them closer, strengthened the bonds that had already joined them. Their love and desire grew deeper.

He moved to the petite line of buttons trailing down her front and began pulling them from their moorings. As he did so, he returned his lips to her throat.

"Your pulse beats so fast, sweet," he murmured.

More buttons were undone, the twain ends of her night rail parting to reveal her breasts. Her breath was coming faster, her sex pulsing and ready, anticipating what would happen next.

"Because I want you," she said.

"You do?" He nipped her flesh, his fingers working on the buttons over her belly now, where there was no discernable difference just yet to show their child grew.

But they both knew.

Rafe's hands were tender as they caressed her there, lingering as they had tended to do ever since she had first divulged the happy news.

"Of course I want you," she told him, breathless.

"How much?" he asked, his left hand moving to her waist and pulling her neatly against him, so that their bodies were flush.

His chest pressed to her back, and the thick hardness of his cock nestled against the cleft of her bottom. As he asked the question, he pulled the last of the buttons free, making her night rail gape.

"Very much," she said, still watching them together in the mirror.

What an erotic picture they made, her handsome husband at her back, his mouth on her neck, biting and sucking, the pale mounds of her breasts revealed, her nipples still scarcely shielded as they tented the fine linen, her sex on display, framed by her thighs.

"If I touch your sweet cunny, will it be dripping for me?" he asked wickedly, his caress trailing lower, but stopping short of where she wanted it most.

"Yes," she said, unable to keep her hips from pumping, seeking his hand.

He kissed her ear, her cheek, and gave her a light pet. Just one sweep of his palm over the curls at the juncture of her thighs. "You are wet, aren't you, lovely?"

He was torturing her. She wanted his fingers on her, in her. But the game itself was almost as delicious as spending. Rafe was an expert at drawing her pleasure to an almost delirious peak before sending her over the edge.

He petted her again, his touch no more than as if it were a feather, passing over her heated flesh. "I didn't hear your answer. Is this pretty cunny of yours wet?"

"Yes," she repeated. "Oh, Rafe. Please. I need you."

He shifted then, hooking the rung of a low stool with his toes and bringing it nearer to her. "Place your foot on the cushion, sweet."

She did as he asked, the movement leaving her thighs parted, the glistening folds of her intimate flesh visible to both their gazes. He hooked his thumbs in the fabric pooled on her shoulders and dragged the night rail down until it fell to the floor with a hushed sound, leaving her completely bare. In the mirror, his gaze traveled over her, searing her as surely as if it were a touch.

"Beautiful," he praised, dropping a kiss on her shoulder. "Touch yourself. Feel how wet you are for me."

Oh heavens. His wicked directive turned the pulsing between her legs into a steady throb. She knew what he wanted, and she wanted it too, though she would have preferred his fingers to her own. Still, her knees trembled as her hand dipped, unerringly finding her pearl. She strummed over the swollen bud, feeling the slickness of her own readiness on her fingertips. Her touches were hesitant at first. She had never touched herself like this as he watched before, and she found the act both shocking and deliciously exciting all at once.

A soft sound of need slipped from her, and she stopped, fingers stilling as her shyness overcame the need for more.

"Don't stop." Rafe kissed her other shoulder, then the hollow behind her ear, his hands caressing paths of fire over her aching breasts, toying with her nipples. "Make yourself come."

His words sent an answering rush of heat to her core. She licked her lips, wondering if she dared to be so bold.

"Don't make me beg, lovely." At her back, he flexed his hips, driving his cock against her bottom. "I want to watch you please yourself."

His tongue traced the whorl of her ear, and her knees

nearly buckled. But he was there, his arm around her waist holding her up, keeping her pressed tightly to his warm strength. She swirled her fingers over her bud, emboldened by his encouragement and the need that was still pulsing inside her. Once, twice, then faster.

"Yes, darling. Just like that," he praised, nipping her earlobe. "Don't stop. Look at yourself, so ready and perfect."

Her senses were sharpened to ultimate alert, and she was aware of everything. His scent enveloping her, his hardness at her back, the warmth of his breath fanning over her throat, her own fingers flying over her flesh, the steady ache building within. In the reflection, her cheeks were flushed, lips parted and dark as if she had been kissed, nipples hard, cunny pink and glistening. She loved the sight of Rafe's hands on her the most, so large and manly, yet touching her with such delicacy.

His left hand glided down her belly as she watched, then grazed over her inner thigh. He found her entrance and plunged two fingers deep inside her, crooking them forward until he found that exquisite place she had never known existed. As she continued pleasuring herself, he fucked in and out of her, bringing her swiftly to bliss.

She cried out, hunching forward, nearly toppling over at the ecstasy. He remained with her, gentling his thrusts, kissing her cheek and whispering words of love to her as he kept her from falling to the floor entirely. Gradually, the ferocity of her climax subsided. Rafe withdrew from her and turned her in his arms, taking her mouth in a slow, lingering kiss, his tongue dipping past her lips to slide against hers.

When he lifted his head, he was breathing as harshly as she was, his expression laden with so much desire and love that she wanted to burst. "Come to the bed with me, sweet. I want to lick you until you spend on my tongue."

Persephone was feeling greedy. She wanted his release as

much, if not more, than her own. He had already left her limp and sated from their play at the mirror.

She opened his banyan and pushed it from his broad shoulders, gratified when he stood before her, splendidly naked, his cock jutting high, a glint of moisture seeping from the crown. The urge to lap it up struck her.

She took him in hand, giving the velvety-smooth length a loving stroke. "I want you in my mouth."

"Ah, God. You'll be the death of me, wife." But he was grinning as he kissed her swiftly once more before taking her hands in his. "Come. I've an idea that will give us both what we want."

He tugged her to the bed and they fell onto it together, kissing passionately, wrapped around each other, their bodies writhing. When he tore his mouth from hers once more, it was to roll away from her and settle on his back.

His big hands grasped her waist. "Turn around and get on your knees, lovely."

Wondering what he was about, she did as he asked, allowing him to guide her until her back faced him and she rested on her knees on the thick, comfortable counterpane.

She glanced at him over her shoulder. "What are we doing?"

"I am going to eat your cunny, and if it pleases you to, you may also suck my cock."

His words made her wetter still, so candid and forbidden.

All she could manage was a one-word response. "Yes."

He positioned her so that she was astride him next, her bottom near to his face. The springy hairs of his chest tickled her inner thighs and the still-pulsing flesh of her sex. It was utterly scandalous.

He stroked her hips. "Give me your cunny, love. I can't wait to taste you."

The need in his voice banished any lingering shyness. She allowed him to help her shift, until...

Oh.

She rested atop him, her belly to his chest, and his tongue was flicking fast and hot and wet over her pearl. Rising toward her was his cock, thick and engorged and within perfect reach of her mouth. She took him in hand, gripping the base, and then lowered her head to run her tongue over his cock head. The taste of him filled her mouth. She flicked her tongue in lingering lashes, licking up every drop as he sucked on her, gorging himself on her cunny as if it were a feast and he was a starving man.

The wet sounds of him pleasuring her mingled with hers, filling the chamber. She took him deep into her throat on a moan, loving the way his hips jerked beneath her. Her ability to give him pleasure was a constant source of wonder to her, and his reaction to her efforts always served to heighten her own desire in return.

His tongue filled her, thrusting in and out as her cunny contracted around him. Already, she was close. He returned to her sensitive clitoris, delivering tender bites that had her riding his face and groaning around his cock. He was slick with her saliva and the precursor to his own spend. She took him deeper, wanting to make him as wild as he was rendering her, sucking and licking and pulling him to the back of her throat, which she knew always brought him so deliciously to the edge.

His hands traveled over her sides, her bottom, branding her, molding her to his touch. On a groan, he held her still for him to flutter little licks over her with gentle pulses before slowly fucking her with his tongue.

She came apart, her release shuddering through her with a violence that took her by surprise. Sparks of light danced behind her eyelids, and she moaned, her mouth full of him, his fingers kneading her hungry flesh as wave after wave of intense pleasure washed over her.

She was boneless, but still intent upon him finding his own release when he pulled her from him, arranging her limp and sated form on the bed. His lips shone with her juices, his cock beautifully erect as he settled between her thighs. She opened wide for him in invitation.

"Come inside me, Rafe."

He gripped his shaft and aligned himself with her aching center. One thrust, and he entered her, the movement fast and sinuous. Leveraging himself on his forearms above her, he began a pace that was fast and furious and everything she wanted. She wrapped her arms and legs around him, body moving in time to his thrusts, urging him on.

She pulled his head down to hers, sealing their lips and sucking her own juices from his tongue. How good he felt inside her. How right. He reached to where they were joined, his fingers working over her pearl until she was coming again, clamping on his cock.

He moaned, his body stiffening, as he finally found his own release, the warm flood of his seed sending another rush of pleasure to her core. He remained where he was, their lips joined, his breathing as harsh as hers, his heart pounding against her breast.

When his head raised, the love in his eyes stole her breath anew. He kissed her nose, his hair tickling her cheeks. "I love you so bleeding much."

She smiled up at him, sweeping an errant curl from his forehead. "I love you every bit as bleeding much, Rafe Sutton."

He grinned, his dimples appearing. "Here now, lovely. I fear I'm debauching you with my wicked ways."

"I know you have," she said softly. "And I love it."

"Good." Still grinning, he kissed her again. "Because I have a lot more debauching to do."

"I am counting upon it, my love," she said against her husband's lips.

~

Thank you for reading Rafe and Persephone's story! I hope you enjoyed it as much as I loved writing it.

Do read on for a bonus excerpt from *Sutton's Surrender*, Book Three in *The Sinful Suttons* series, featuring the adventurous Miss Pen Sutton and the proper, icy Garrick Weir, Lord Lindsey. Is there any hope for the rigid son of a duke and an East End lady?

Please consider leaving an honest review of *Sutton's Sins*. Reviews are greatly appreciated! If you'd like to keep up to date with my latest releases and series news, sign up for my newsletter here or follow me on Amazon or BookBub. Join my reader's group on Facebook for bonus content, early excerpts, giveaways, and more.

~

Sutton's Surrender
The Sinful Suttons
Book Three

With his impeccable reputation and undeniable good looks, Garrick Weir, Viscount Lindsey, heir to the Duke of Dresden, has earned his place at the apex of fashionable London society. Every lady on the marriage mart wants him as her prize, and every young fop wants to be him. When his foolish younger brother declares his intention to marry a devious East End fortune hunter, Garrick is appalled. He vows to do everything in his power to stop the mésalliance from occurring.

Penelope Sutton has long considered Lord Aidan Weir her unlikely friend. But when he decides he wants to marry her to anger his father and condescending brother, she refuses to take part in his schemes. She would have told the arrogant Lord Lindsey as much had he not attempted to bribe her. And she *most definitely* would have informed him he should take his blunt back to Mayfair where it, and he, belongs...had he not kissed her.

Torn between a confounding attraction to Miss Sutton and the desire to make certain she stays far, far away from his brother, Garrick must prove she is every bit the title-hungry fortune seeker he believes her to be. Pen is equally determined to show the viscount how very wrong he is about her. But when their battle leads to much higher stakes than pride, everything changes for the rigidly proper lord and the rookeries-born lady.

∾

Chapter One
London, 1816

Garrick Weir, Viscount Lindsey, heir to the Duke of Dresden, had ventured to the East End with his outrage, an unwise proliferation of coin, and the determination to pay off the scheming, fortune-hunting harlot who was attempting to ensnare his madcap younger brother into matrimony. Thus far, he had managed to avoid pickpockets and other would-be criminals. He had similarly surpassed guards and found his way, unscathed, to the private room where his quarry would be found within the next half hour. The palms he had greased on his way here had suggested she would be within shortly.

Tallying ledgers.

Apparently, the lowborn miscreant was intelligent enough to know her arithmetic, at least—if his study of the neatly penned sums before him was to be trusted—in the case of gin being purchased versus consumed by patrons. But then, one could only suppose she also possessed enough intellect to bamboozle his idiotic sibling.

To be fair, Aidan was a stripling who thought with his cock and little else. It was entirely likely all that was required to persuade him was a set of breasts and a willing cunny.

Garrick shuddered as he thought of his brother's appalling lack of judgment and turned the page in the ledger. Aidan had made it more than clear he did not give a farthing about preserving the Weir family name. Never mind that the Duke of Dresden was one of the oldest, most revered titles in England. Being a part of such a distinguished lineage was not sufficient for Aidan, who amused himself besmirching their good name by drinking, whoring, gambling, gadding about at bareknuckle boxing matches, and announcing he intended to marry a lowborn title seeker.

His pronouncement at dinner the evening before had been the ultimate slap to the face for their father. The duke suffered from a weak heart, and Garrick had feared their father would expire at the table from the fury which had overtaken him. Garrick and his other brother Jonathan did not fault their father for his outrage. Miss Penelope Sutton was the most unsuitable match Aidan could have found, save from a Covent Garden doxy. Mother had called for her hartshorn and retired to her apartments.

Garrick sifted a few more pages of the ledger, his *ennui* leading him to grudgingly admit Miss Sutton's penmanship was tidy and concise. Her spelling was regular. Perhaps she had received *some* manner of education. Not that such a matter should concern him. After this evening, he would neither see the woman nor hear from her ever again.

A sound in the hall beyond interrupted his perusal. He straightened, moving away from the desk and assuming his most intimidating pose as the door opened. She was earlier than he had expected, but it was just as well. The sooner they could settle this disagreeable matter, the better. He had a ball to attend.

The woman standing before Garrick took him by surprise. He had imagined she would be dressed in an unseemly display, breasts nearly popping from her bodice, her gown dampened to render it sheer. But instead, she wore a modest affair of an indeterminate light hue, buttoned to the throat. Her auburn hair was bound in a simple knot, a few tendrils free to frame her face.

"Who are you?" she demanded.

Well, her rudeness certainly met—*and surpassed*—his expectations.

He bowed as if they were in a drawing room rather than a ramshackle East End gaming hell where countless despicable acts of gambling, drinking to excess, and Lord knew what else had occurred. "I am Lord Lindsey, Miss Sutton."

She remained where she was, pinning him with a narrow, hazel-eyed stare. "Am I meant to know you?"

He tamped down a surge of irritation. *Everyone* knew him.

But then, she was a little no one, wasn't she?

"You are acquainted with my brother, Lord Aidan Weir," he elaborated grimly, for he refused to acknowledge the supposed betrothal between herself and his sibling.

The marriage was never happening, and he had lowered

himself to visit this intolerable haven of iniquity to make certain of that.

A frown marred her otherwise fine features. "You are Aidan's brother?"

Garrick grudgingly noted Miss Penelope Sutton was quite beautiful. Scarcely any wonder his scapegrace of a brother had been following her about these last few months, sniffing at her skirts.

"I am *Lord* Aidan's brother, as I said," he repeated, emphasizing his brother's title.

The familiarity of his sibling's name on her lips was irksome, and not just for the obvious reason.

"*Lord* Aidan." She was unsmiling, her gaze studying him from head to toe in rude fashion as she remained where she was. "Yes, of course. Forgive me for forgetting he has a brother. He does not often speak of his family."

Was that meant to be a barb? And why had the witch yet to curtsy and show the deference which was due him?

"I do not suppose he would," Garrick commented mildly. "Do you intend to hover on the threshold all evening, or will you enter, Miss Sutton?"

He was growing weary of this game. An evening of entertainment beckoned, and he did not like the manner in which his body was reacting to this brazen chit. He was far too aware of her, his entire being acutely on edge.

Anger, he told himself. That was all it was.

She is an East End fortune hunter greedy to snatch a titled gentleman as her marital prize.

But she was a lovely one, and he could not deny it, much as that fact aggrieved him.

"Why have you come?" she asked instead of answering the question he had posed, still motionless.

She looked like a frightened doe, poised for flight.

He sighed. "Miss Sutton, enter the room, if you please. I

hardly wish for all the world to hear my private affairs. Whilst my brother does not have a care for discretion, I do, and that is why I have sought you out this evening."

"Has something happened to him?" She stepped over the threshold at last, the door not entirely closing at her back.

It would have to suffice.

"Your concern is almost touching, Miss Sutton." He strode forward, eliminating the distance separating them. "But then, I suppose any title-greedy viper would be similarly worried at the prospect of losing the lord she believes she has ensnared."

"Are you daring to insult me in my own family's establishment, my lord?"

"I speak truth." Curse it, was that her scent reaching him just now? She smelled like a walk in a summer's meadow, fresh with a hint of a floral note.

East End fortune hunters were not meant to smell so luscious.

What the devil ails you? This is the woman Aidan has been chasing. And, knowing Aidan, bedding.

He disgusted himself. And yet, the woman before him possessed a certain attraction he could not deny. Not just her fine features or the vibrant warmth of her hair, but the manner in which she carried herself. He had no doubt, were she to stand in a ballroom, she would command the attention of every gentleman in the chamber.

"What truth do you speak, sir?" Her full lips compressed with disapproval.

Ah, a rarity, that. A woman who looked upon him as if he were disagreeable to behold. How intriguing. He could not recall the last time a lady had gazed at him with anything other than admiration, whether genuine or manufactured.

"That you are a title-greedy viper. It is to be expected of a lady in your unfortunate circumstances." He clenched his hands at his sides to keep from giving in to the urge to brush a stray wisp of hair from her cheek. "But I have come prepared to give you what you truly wish. How much do you require to leave my brother alone and end this nonsensical betrothal?"

Her eyes, a curious shade of green and gray with flecks of cinnamon, and fringed with generous lashes, widened. "Are you bribing me, my lord?"

"Yes," he said without hesitation. "I am."

Want more? Get *Sutton's Surrender* now!

AUTHOR'S NOTE

The cant speech used by the Suttons has been sourced mostly from *The Memoirs of James Hardy Vaux* (1819) and Grose's *Dictionary of the Vulgar Tongue* (1811). In case you were wondering, the words *screw* and *shag*, which we tend to think of as modernisms, both appear in the latter, defined as "to copulate." The word "scrope" is cant for *farthing*.

DON'T MISS SCARLETT'S OTHER ROMANCES!

Complete Book List
HISTORICAL ROMANCE

Heart's Temptation
A Mad Passion (Book One)
Rebel Love (Book Two)
Reckless Need (Book Three)
Sweet Scandal (Book Four)
Restless Rake (Book Five)
Darling Duke (Book Six)
The Night Before Scandal (Book Seven)

Wicked Husbands
Her Errant Earl (Book One)
Her Lovestruck Lord (Book Two)
Her Reformed Rake (Book Three)
Her Deceptive Duke (Book Four)
Her Missing Marquess (Book Five)
Her Virtuous Viscount (Book Six)

League of Dukes
Nobody's Duke (Book One)
Heartless Duke (Book Two)
Dangerous Duke (Book Three)
Shameless Duke (Book Four)
Scandalous Duke (Book Five)
Fearless Duke (Book Six)

Notorious Ladies of London
Lady Ruthless (Book One)
Lady Wallflower (Book Two)
Lady Reckless (Book Three)
Lady Wicked (Book Four)
Lady Lawless (Book Five)
Lady Brazen (Book 6)

Unexpected Lords
The Detective Duke (Book One)
The Playboy Peer (Book Two)

The Wicked Winters
Wicked in Winter (Book One)
Wedded in Winter (Book Two)
Wanton in Winter (Book Three)
Wishes in Winter (Book 3.5)
Willful in Winter (Book Four)
Wagered in Winter (Book Five)
Wild in Winter (Book Six)
Wooed in Winter (Book Seven)
Winter's Wallflower (Book Eight)
Winter's Woman (Book Nine)
Winter's Whispers (Book Ten)
Winter's Waltz (Book Eleven)
Winter's Widow (Book Twelve)

Winter's Warrior (Book Thirteen)

The Sinful Suttons
Sutton's Spinster (Book One)
Sutton's Sins (Book Two)
Sutton's Surrender (Book Three)

Sins and Scoundrels
Duke of Depravity
Prince of Persuasion
Marquess of Mayhem
Sarah
Earl of Every Sin
Duke of Debauchery

Second Chance Manor
The Matchmaker and the Marquess by Scarlett Scott
The Angel and the Aristocrat *by Merry Farmer*
The Scholar and the Scot *by Caroline Lee*
The Venus and the Viscount by Scarlett Scott
The Buccaneer and the Bastard *by Merry Farmer*
The Doxy and the Duke *by Caroline Lee*

Stand-alone Novella
Lord of Pirates

CONTEMPORARY ROMANCE
Love's Second Chance
Reprieve (Book One)
Perfect Persuasion (Book Two)
Win My Love (Book Three)

Coastal Heat
Loved Up (Book One)

ABOUT THE AUTHOR

USA Today and Amazon bestselling author Scarlett Scott writes steamy Victorian and Regency romance with strong, intelligent heroines and sexy alpha heroes. She lives in Pennsylvania and Maryland with her Canadian husband, adorable identical twins, and two dogs.

A self-professed literary junkie and nerd, she loves reading anything, but especially romance novels, poetry, and Middle English verse. Catch up with her on her website http://www.scarlettscottauthor.com/. Hearing from readers never fails to make her day.

Scarlett's complete book list and information about upcoming releases can be found at http://www.scarlettscottauthor.com/.

Connect with Scarlett! You can find her here:
    Join Scarlett Scott's reader group on Facebook for early excerpts, giveaways, and a whole lot of fun!
    Sign up for her newsletter here
    https://www.tiktok.com/@authorscarlettscott